Hawker blasted open the door of the headquarters of the Panthers, one of L.A.'s most vicious street gangs. He moved in, saw two men, and shouted, "Freeze! I'll blow your heads off if you so much as blink. Now toss those weapons away."

The man who'd carried the shotgun said, "You're the dude who wasted Fat Albert and Spooky, and shot Cat Man. You're dead, boy. Right now you're breathin' and your heart's beating, but you're a goner."

Hawker glanced over his shoulder. A hugely fat black man filled the doorway. He dwarfed the revolver in his right hand. Hawker let the Colt Commander fall by his feet.

The shotgun man chuckled and looked at the others. "Might as well have some fun before he die, eh, fellas?"

Hawker had launched the attack, but could he survive the . . .

L.A. WARS

L.A. WARS

Carl Ramm

Carl Ramm (signature)

A DELL BOOK

Published by
Dell Publishing Co., Inc.
1 Dag Hammarskjold Plaza
New York, New York 10017

Dell ® TM 681510, Dell Publishing Co., Inc.

ISBN: 0-440-14645-3

Printed in the United States of America

First printing—June 1984

one

James Hawker found the girl's body in the alley between an abandoned Sears store and a pawnshop.

Starnsdale had once been a community of struggling actors, writers, and stuntmen. Now it was a ghetto. A slum. No one struggled anymore. They lived. They rotted. They died.

Hawker had been traveling from one roof to another, above the streets.

When he noticed the curl of pale hair and the limp, white hand protruding from beneath the trash, he climbed down a fire escape ladder.

A cat screamed and ricocheted from a cardboard box toward the street. The alley smelled of garbage and sour urine.

It was one fourteen A.M.

The blue glare of the streetlight showed a decrepit Cadillac beyond the mouth of the alley. It rested on cement blocks in lieu of tires. Its windows were shattered. Someone had splashed the word PANTHERS in black paint on the side. The Cadillac looked like some strange steel animal, tortured beyond hope.

Hawker slid the little Ingram submachine gun off his shoulder and hung it by its sling on the ladder. The long, tubular silencer—almost as long as the Ingram—weighted the muzzle toward the tarmac.

He began pulling garbage and trash away from the body. What he saw sickened him.

He knew the girl to be seventeen. She looked younger. She had a thin, angular face with high, hollow cheeks. A purple bruise bloated the left side of her jaw.

The hair was a mousy brown, but had been tinted blond—as if bleached by the sun. In California everyone wanted to be a surf god or a surf goddess.

Her blue eyes were wide with the horror of her death, her thin lips drawn back into a silent scream.

She had not died easily. Or prettily. She had suffered all the terrors and indignities of which nightmares are made.

Her killers had stripped her naked.

Her breasts were small, pale cones, like those of an adolescent. They had used a knife or a razor on one breast. Blood had coagulated around the initial *P* they had carved into her.

A pair of sheer panties remained around one thin ankle. Her legs had been forced apart, and more blood had coagulated on her thighs and beneath her.

The blood had a dull metallic stink.

James Hawker stood, feeling the anger move through him like nausea. Fifteen miles away tourists probably still roamed the star-haunted streets of Hollywood. A few miles beyond that, California's rich slept soundly in their Beverly Hills fortresses.

But here, in the bowels of this south Los Angeles hellhole, the animals were allowed to roam and steal and murder and rape.

A few blocks away, Hawker knew, a man and woman were not sleeping.

He could picture them in the living room of their neat stucco Spanish-style home in the last respectable neighborhood left in Starnsdale. This lone neighborhood was known as Hillsboro, because of the main street which ribboned through it.

Slowly, lethally, Starnsdale had followed the footsteps of so many other suburban communities. The middle-income areas had gradually become lower-income areas and, finally, ghettos.

The ghettos produced a few people smart enough and determined enough to work their way toward a better life. But, mostly, the Starnsdale ghetto produced drunks, drug addicts, whores and—worst of all—savage bands of street gangs.

The people of Hillsboro had watched with concern, and then terror, as their middle-class neighborhood shrank to a narrow peninsula of respectability surrounded by a sea of ghetto violence.

Hawker could imagine the man and woman in their neat stucco home exchanging nervous glances, and a few nervous words.

The ticking of the clock on the wall would be like a hammer in their ears.

This girl was their daughter.

Hawker wished he had a jacket or a sheet with which to cover the body before he notified the police.

He decided to use his black T-shirt for want of anything better. She had already suffered enough indignity.

He pulled it over his head and draped it over the girl's face and chest, like a shroud.

"*Hey . . . white boy!*"

Hawker whirled to see four figures silhouetted by the streetlight. They stood at the mouth of the alley.

"What you be doin' on Panther turf, white boy? You lost? Some mean ol' nigger steal your car or rob you or something? Aw, poor little white boy done lost, fellas." There was thick laughter as they approached, walking in a line toward him.

Hawker rested his hands easily on his hips. "A girl's been murdered here," he said between tight lips. "And unless you assholes want to join her, you'd better freeze right there while I go for the cops. Got it?"

The force of his voice stopped them for a moment. Hawker could see them more clearly: four black men, all in their late teens or early twenties. They wore jeans, dark T-shirts, and base-

ball caps with the bills flipped upward. Around
their necks, in the style sported by late-show
cowboys, were tied blue and black bandannas.

It was the standard uniform of the Starns
Panthers, one of Starnsdale's most violent street
gangs.

"Ohh, this white boy be *bad*!" the tallest of the
four joked in mock terror. The others laughed and
slapped outstretched hands.

"We goin' to kill him, Cat Man?" another asked.

The tall one, Cat Man, grimaced as if the question was stupid. "What you think, motherfucker?
This white boy done found the girl. Then he see
us in the alley. Cops be tracking our asses for the
next month if he gets away and squeals to them."

"You killed her?" Hawker whispered.

Cat Man held his arms outstretched, smiling,
and dipped slightly. It was like a regal bow. "The
Panthers tried to show the lady a very nice time.
Tried to show the lady how to get down, Panther-
fashion. Dig? The lady couldn't find the groove,
man, couldn't go with the flow." The wide, white
grin disappeared from Cat Man's face. "So we
each took our turns, then branded the bitch and
killed her." His hand searched the back of his
pants momentarily, reappearing with a stub-nosed
.38. Its nickel-plated barrel looked black in the
poor light of the alley.

"Now the Panthers are going to get down with
you, white boy," Cat Man said, his face contorted
into a snarl. Two others had drawn small handguns,
and Cat Man tossed his .38 to a short, overweight

kid to his right. "Hold my piece, Fat Albert, while I do my thing on this Casper. I'm gonna show you the way to hell, white boy. I'm gonna kill you with my hands."

Cat Man was well named. He was smooth and fast—but he was too anxious. He took two bobbing steps, then lunged at Hawker with a sizzling fist.

Hawker stepped under it, then cut Cat Man's face open with a jarring series of rights and lefts. As he began to fall, Hawker grabbed Cat Man's bandanna and swung him toward the other three to give himself enough time to reach the Ingram submachine gun.

Two shots exploded, and lead splattered off brick above Hawker's head, stinging his face.

He swept the Ingram into his arms, dived, rolled, and fired. The silencer reduced the chain-rattle clatter of the submachine gun to a series of heavy thudding noises.

The three Panthers jolted one by one. They backpedaled against the walls, hands clawing desperately at their faces and their chests.

Fat Albert, his jaw shot away, sat heavily on the tarmac, a stunned expression in his eyes. Whimpering, he leaned against the wall of the pawnshop. His head slumped.

Like the other two, he was dead.

Hawker got quickly to his feet. He took his T-shirt from the body of the dead girl, then went to the corpse of Fat Albert. The stub-nosed .38 was still locked in his hand. Hawker pried it loose.

He found a chunk of gravel and studied the bare brick wall for a moment. In one flowing motion he drew the head of a giant hawk, and added a fierce eye. Beneath it, in block letters, he wrote: REVENGE.

Out on the street there was the sound of voices. Hawker knew he had to hurry.

Cat Man was just waking up, trying groggily to figure out what had happened. Using the T-shirt, Hawker wiped his own prints from the Ingram and placed it beside Cat Man.

Cat Man's eyes widened as he saw the corpses of his three dead friends. "Motherfu—*you killed 'em all!* Razor gonna get you for this, man. Razor gonna have your head for this!"

Hawker's smile was bitter. He swung the .38 easily in his hand, wondering who Razor was. The Panthers' leader? Probably. "I didn't kill anybody," Hawker said calmly. "Not as far as the cops are concerned, anyway. They'll think you did it. And lab reports from the girl's body will give them enough evidence to make any charge stick." Hawker motioned with his head toward the Ingram. "Now go for it, asshole. Go for the gun before I kill you. I'm giving you a chance."

Cat Man tried to crawl away, his voice high-pitched, crying. "Don't be killin' me, mister. Shit, this ain't legal. I got my rights, man. I know my fucking rights—"

"Go for the gun!" Hawker shouted in a whisper.

Cat Man's hands were a blur as they reached for the Ingram. The moment his fingers were around the metal trigger, though, Hawker pressed the .38 to Cat Man's temple.

"Oh, God," Cat Man whimpered. "I'll do anything, man, do anything you want me to do. Just don't kill me."

"Yeah. There is something you can do," Hawker said as he pulled the hammer back. "Tell your slimy street gang friends what happened here. The cops won't believe you, but your buddies will. And tell your buddy Razor I'm just getting started."

Without warning Hawker swung the barrel of the revolver from Cat Man's head to Cat Man's groin. He pulled the trigger and jumped away from the spout of blood, as Cat Man writhed on the tarmac, screaming.

Hawker wiped the .38 clean and pressed it back into Fat Albert's right hand. Then, taking care not to touch the revolver, Hawker scraped Fat Albert's knuckles raw on the asphalt and touched them with Cat Man's blood.

It would explain the cuts on Cat Man's face.

The dead girl looked pitifully pale and small amid the corpses of the animals who had murdered her. Hawker wished there were some way he could sweep her away from all this. He couldn't spare her parents the knowledge of her death, but he wished there was some way to spare them the circumstances of her dying.

Unfortunately, there wasn't.

Not any longer.

There were more voices on the street now, and the clatter of people running.

Hawker threw the T-shirt over his shoulder and pulled the black watch-cap low over his forehead. He studied the alley for a moment, making sure he had left no footprints in the blood.

He hadn't.

As Cat Man screamed, James Hawker vanished up the fire escape.

two

Four days earlier Jacob Montgomery Hayes had
summoned Hawker to his sprawling Kenilworth
estate on the shore of Lake Michigan. As usual he
had sent a messenger boy.

"Have a project which may interest you," the
note read. *"Will warn you beforehand that it could
be tougher than the Florida project."*

Hayes was referring to their first experimental
vigilante mission. On a small island on the west
coast of Florida, Hawker had slammed head-on
with a South American organization hell-bent on
ruining America's economy.

Hawker had left a lot of corpses in his wake.
But the mission was a success. Now Hayes, one of
the richest men in the world, was summoning
Hawker for a second job.

And James Hawker was more than ready. He

had spent a boring three months waiting. He had done everything he could to stay busy: refining his computer techniques, sparring at the old Bridgeport gym on Chicago's south side, forcing his body through a daily running and calisthenic routine that would have wearied a Spartan.

So Hawker welcomed the summons, welcomed, once again, the chance to put his cop's instincts and skills to work—and put his life on the line one more time.

On a bright June afternoon he had climbed into his vintage midnight-blue Corvette and caught the Kennedy Expressway northward, toward Kenilworth.

Hayes Hill, shielded from the rest of the world by a high wrought-iron fence and twenty acres of rolling park, was a red-brick fortress through the summer trees.

The electronic gate swung open at Hawker's approach, then swung closed behind him as he wound his way down the narrow asphalt drive.

In the distance Lake Michigan shimmered like liquid sky.

Jacob Montgomery Hayes's formal English butler, Hendricks, let Hawker in.

"Mr. Hayes told me to come over, Hendricks."

"What a novel way of saying you have an appointment."

Hawker smiled. Hendricks was right out of a 1940s English movie, and he had a wicked sense of humor.

Hawker decided he could joke, too. "Hendricks—

Mr. Hayes told me that you were a British spy during the war. MI-6. Espionage. What about it?"

For just a moment the butler's eyes flickered—he'd been caught off-guard. He soon recovered. "Men found a great many things to be done during the war, sir. We were among the very few who did not catch a venereal disease in the process."

"Does that mean you were a spy?" insisted Hawker, grinning.

"On the contrary, sir. It means we wore our condoms like proper Englishmen. Steel yourself, sir. Mr. Hayes will think you've gone quite mad, laughing like that."

Hayes was in his study. He was a stocky, middle-sized man, with wire-rimmed glasses and a fierce, honest face. Surprisingly, he wore a knit pullover shirt and a long-brimmed fishing cap.

He sat at a cherrywood desk near the massive stone fireplace. A breeze came through the window, moving the curtains. He was hunched over a thin vise, tying a fly. A briar pipe was clenched between his teeth.

He looked up only briefly when Hawker entered, then returned to his work. Hawker stood over his shoulder, watching him wrap green Swannundaze over white goose biots.

"A trout fly?" Hawker, who liked to fish, asked.

"Right. An Aigner peacock nymph."

"Ah."

"I didn't know you tied, James."

"I don't. Not well, anyway. Sometimes I say 'ah' to pretend I understand when I really don't."

Jacob Hayes chuckled. Finished, he shoved himself away from the desk and motioned Hawker into a leather chair. Looking beyond Hayes's shoulder, Hawker could see an oil portrait of a yellow Labrador retriever, the gun cabinet filled with classic field guns, and a wall full of books.

"You've recovered from the Mahogany Key mission?" Hayes asked without preamble.

Hawker nodded.

"What do you know about California?"

"Not much. Let's see . . . the Beach Boys, Hollywood, earthquakes, Cannery Row, cocaine—"

"And street gangs," Hayes interrupted. He pulled a file out of the desk and handed it to Hawker.

"Street gangs, as in *West Side Story?*"

Hawker was being facetious, and Hayes allowed a thin smile to cross his face. "Not exactly. I'm talking about Los Angeles street gangs. They don't have much time for singing and dancing. They're too busy blasting each other in the back with shotguns. Or beating up pedestrians. Or cutting the throats of the people they rob."

Hawker opened the file as Hayes continued to talk. "There's a suburban community south of L.A. called Starnsdale. It used to be a nice place. A lot of minor actors and scriptwriters used to live there. It had some light industry. Good stores. Nice churches."

"Sounds like Bridgeport," Hawker said. He was referring to Chicago's Irish section, where he had grown up.

"Exactly. And just about the same thing happened. As the houses on the outskirts of Starnsdale aged, the wrong kind of people started moving in. It got worse and worse. The community began to rot at the edges. Soon they became full-fledged ghettos."

"And now?"

"Now Starnsdale has one little strip of area, known as Hillsboro, which hasn't been taken over yet. The people in Hillsboro are the last holdouts. But they live in absolute terror. Within a ten-mile radius of Starnsdale there are fifty-seven different black and Hispanic gangs. It's been estimated they are responsible for nearly five hundred murders a year—half of those through gang warfare. They roam the streets at night like wolves. No one and nothing is safe in their path."

"I'm surprised the people who live there haven't sold their homes and moved."

"Would you buy a house in a place like Hillsboro? No. No sane person would. They can't move because they can't sell. These people are trapped, James. They live on a narrow peninsula of sanity surrounded by violence. But they want to fight back.

"Last year they organized a neighborhood watch program. But they were poorly equipped and poorly trained. They had a couple of minor confrontations with the two toughest gangs in the area and fared disastrously. In fact the gangs were so enraged by the confrontations, they've been systematically taking revenge on the neighborhood watch members ever since."

Hayes leaned forward slightly, his big hands braced on the arms of the chair. "I want you to stop it, James. I want you to fly to L.A. and help the people of Hillsboro. The police have tried, but, as you well know, manpower and resources are never sufficient in a large city. Plus, you will have the advantage of being able to work outside the legal system. These gang members are brutal, James, and brutal methods will have to be used."

"It's a double-edged sword," said Hawker. "The gang members will be after me from one side, the cops from the other."

"There are names of people to contact in the file." Jacob Montgomery Hayes stood and held out his hand. "As before, I will supply whatever you need for the job. Except safety. I can't provide that. Be careful, James. Don't get caught. You understand my meaning?"

"Ah," said James Hawker. "I do."

Three days later Hawker descended through the clouds of the San Gabriel Mountains, and then the smog of L.A., landing at Los Angeles International Airport.

From the air the city spread away like a Monopoly board ablaze. He had never seen so many cars in such frantic motion.

Hawker rented a new Cutlass at the Hertz desk and used his pocket road-map to spirit him through the traffic jams and bustle to the San Diego Freeway—where there was an even worse traffic jam, and more bustle.

The air was like acid. The sun glimmered through the carbon monoxide fumes like a yellow light bulb. People screamed at each other from convertibles and flipped hand signs from low-slung Mercedes.

At the Manhattan Beach exit Hawker got off and headed east along Route 91, through the Quick Shop, topless bar and dimestore clutter of Torrance and Carson.

The ghettos began in Compton: broken windows, junked cars, and winos.

The few businesses that remained open were barred and locked like penal institutions.

It didn't get any better when he crossed into the corporate limits of Starnsdale. Bands of men and women roamed the streets in sweat-stained clothes, carrying bottles in brown bags. The streets were littered with trash. Emaciated dogs slept in the sun while winos curled up in the shade.

Two words were repeated over and over in the street graffiti: PANTHERS and SATANÁS.

The words were splashed on everything. Building walls. Stop signs. Cars and windows.

Panthers was always written in black, *Satanás* in red.

The slums of Starnsdale changed abruptly as he turned onto Hillsboro Boulevard. Homes here were well kept, neat stucco and wood buildings with hedges and verandas. Palm trees grew in the middle of the boulevard, and sprinkler systems waved water over mown lawns.

Hawker had to turn around twice before he found the proper address. It was a small Spanish-

style home with a smaller courtyard. Hawker noticed the bars on the windows and the alarm system
wires as he knocked.

"Mr. Kahl? Virgil Kahl?"

"Yes?" A thin, ascetic man stood in the doorway,
a book in one hand, a pair of bifocals in the other.
Hawker guessed him to be about fifty-five.

"Jacob Montgomery Hayes suggested I contact
you."

"Hayes? Oh! Jake Hayes!" A shy grin flashed on
the man's face. "Come on in . . ."

"Hawker. James Hawker."

"Come right on in, Mr. Hawker. We weren't
expecting you so soon."

Hawker followed him into a well-furnished living room lined with more books. On the wall were
several photographs of Kahl with well-known stars
of the fifties and sixties. Hayes's file had told
Hawker that Kahl was the organizer of the Hillsboro neighborhood watch program. It hadn't told
him Kahl's occupation.

"Are you an actor, Mr. Kahl?"

The man's smile widened. "Good God, no—and
call me Virgil, please. No, no, I'm a scriptwriter. I
used to do quite a few film projects, but I'm afraid
my stuff has gone out of style with the younger
producers. Now I do free-lance television work."

"Sounds interesting."

"Only if you like to sit in front of a typewriter
day after day." Kahl brushed his thin hair back, as
if anxious to abandon conversational pleasantries.
He put on his glasses and sat up straight. "So!

Jake Hayes says you're here to help us get the neighborhood watch going again."

"That's right. I'm at your full disposal."

"I'm afraid it's not going to be easy, Mr. Hawker. Our last outing was not very successful. Two other men and I were badly beaten. That was six months ago. I spent a week in the hospital. Since that time a member of our watch group was murdered. His throat was slit with a razor. Two other members have had their houses burned."

"The street gangs play rough."

"Rough? Why, they're absolute savages," Kahl said bitterly. "We're not safe on the streets; we're not safe in our homes, for God's sake."

"Which of the gangs has been taking revenge on you?"

Kahl made a helpless motion with his hands. "Who can say for sure? The Panthers is a gang comprised mostly of blacks. They wear blue and black bandannas. The Satanás is mostly Latin. They wear red bandannas. One's as bad as the other. They're both killers."

"Your watch group had confrontations with both of them?"

"Yes. And did badly each time." Kahl dropped his book on the desk wearily. He looked at Hawker, as if trying to make him understand why he felt so defeated. "We thought our main strength as a group was our brains and our organizational ability. But during each confrontation they just completely overpowered us. We didn't have a chance."

"The gangs are comprised mostly of kids? Teen-agers?"

"That's an interesting point. Most of the active members—the ones you see wearing their ban-dannas on the streets—are almost all teen-agers. But I know for a fact that they get backing from adults. Full-fledged criminals. They use the kids to do their dirty work. Under the banner of gang loyalty the kids will kill, steal, anything. The adults sit back, keep their hands clean, and collect the money."

"Who told you that?"

"One of the detectives in the Los Angeles Po-lice Department."

"The police are still trying to help you?"

"As much as they can—which isn't all that much. There are a great many street gangs in the City of Angels, Mr. Hawker. It would take an army of policemen to keep them under control. In other words we welcome your offer to help."

"I'll do everything I can, Virgil," Hawker said. "And I guess the best way to begin is to get a little more information. All gangs have headquarters, Virgil. Do you know where the Panthers and Satanás meet?"

"The Panthers, of course, hang out in the black section. That would be between Rosencratz and Blitz streets. The Satanás are on the other side of Hillsboro—the east side—on Ybor Avenue. I don't know any specific addresses."

"Do the two gangs ever operate together? Do they get along?"

Kahl snorted. "Like fire and water. They kill more of their own kind than they do honest citizens—and our thanks for that. They call it 'gang-banging.'" Kahl leaned forward to make an important point. "I've spent considerable time studying these groups, Mr. Hawker—"

"James."

"James it is, then." Kahl smiled. "I've watched and read extensively, trying to learn what makes these street gangs tick. I knew their activities resembled those of some other groups I've read about, but it took me a while to put my finger on it." Kahl poked at his glasses. "Have you ever read some of the early observations on aboriginal behavior in Africa?"

"Do Tarzan movies count?"

"Oddly enough, yes. The aborigines in both history and fiction put great store in tribesmanship. They both love colorful, gaudy costumes, and they take special care in selecting or awarding nicknames. Both take pride in the theatrics they can lend to warfare—gang members call it being 'cool.' Street gangs like to give their violence a style, a flair. The more unusual the form of violence, the better.

"You see," he continued, "they are superstitious in that what they don't understand either infuriates them or terrifies them. They function on emotion, not intellect. I think it might be the one chink in their armor, James. They are brutal and fearless because they never have to fight alone. They can't be reasoned with, because they seem

to lack any suggestion of morality. They understand only two things: violence and fear."

"So you're saying the best way to beat them is
to scare them?"

Kahl nodded quickly. "If we could just *find*
some way to scare them. They laugh at police.
And they actually seem to take pride in being
arrested—perhaps because so few of them are ever
sent to prison."

"It's not going to be easy, then," said Hawker,
deep in thought, an absent expression on his face.
He sat silent for a time, then his face slowly
lightened. "But maybe . . . maybe it won't be
quite as hard to scare them as we think." He stood
up quickly. "Do you think we could get your
watch group together tomorrow night?"

Kahl made a noncommittal gesture. "I can try.
Most of them are ready to give up. Can I call you
and let you know in the morning?"

"Jacob Hayes rented a house for me on Manhattan Beach. I don't know the telephone number
yet—"

Hawker was interrupted by a handsome, older
woman's rushing into the room. She had flaxen
hair edged with gray and a plain, librarianlike
face. She seemed surprised that her husband had
company. Her hands were pressed together nervously, and her eyes showed concern. She looked
from Kahl to Hawker, and then back to her
husband. "Virgil," she said anxiously. "I hate to
interrupt, but Julie seems to be . . . missing. She
was supposed to be home by three, and I've just

finished calling all her friends. . . ." Mrs. Kahl choked momentarily, near tears.

Kahl tried to make light of it. Julie was his teen-age daughter, he explained. She had gone to her summer-school class, and probably decided to go to a movie, he reasoned. But the worry was evident on his face.

There was a big Seth Thomas grandfather clock in a corner of the living room, ticking the seconds away.

It was six fifteen P.M.

Hawker excused himself as they dialed the police.

Virgil Kahl's hand shook as he held the telephone.

Hawker didn't feel like waiting for official help. He drove to Manhattan Beach, found his rental house, showered, changed into jeans, a black T-shirt, and black cap. From one of the crates Jacob Hayes had shipped to the house, Hawker selected a few pieces of weaponry and hid them in the car with two changes of clothes.

At first dark he headed for the slums of the street gangs.

He would search for more than five hours before finding the body of Julie Kahl. . . .

three

As Hawker disappeared up the fire escape ladder, sirens wailed in the distance.

The sirens mixed with the echoing screams of Cat Man.

Hawker doubted that Cat Man would die. But he would spend a lifetime wishing that he had. And he would never rape again. Ever.

Almost as important, Cat Man would spread the word. His tribesmen would visit him in the hospital, or in jail, and he would whisper the truth to them. He would tell them about the lone red-haired man who killed just as quickly and just as brutally as the most savage street fighter.

Virgil Kahl's theory had struck a chord in Hawker. The street gangs liked violence with a flair, he had said. It was the one thing they would both admire and fear.

Hawker would give them plenty to fear. And he would start building his reputation.

Tonight.

Hawker made his way across the tops of the buildings. Occasionally he had to make a long jump from one rooftop to another. Twice he interrupted teen-agers in feverish copulation.

Below him, on the streets, neon signs flashed garishly, red and green. Customized cars prowled, polished like gems. At stoplights drivers revved their engines. The fronts of the cars bounced like rearing horses.

Low riders.

Hawker wondered why California was the birthplace of so many strange fads.

Perhaps it was boredom. Or the acid air. Or something in the water. Somewhere Hawker had read that trout raised in hatcheries had to be gradually introduced to acids and aluminum before being released in polluted lakes. It was the only way they would survive.

Life forms can live in poison—as long as they are poisoned slowly.

Los Angeles seemed the perfect proving ground.

Hawker moved on through the shadows.

It took him nearly an hour to work his way back to his car. He got in and drove slowly through Hillsboro. A police car sat outside Virgil Kahl's home. A cop stood in the doorway. Hawker knew he had been burdened with the duty every cop dreads: breaking the news of a death in the family.

Hawker barely knew the Kahls, but already he mourned for them. They seemed like a nice couple. And now their every waking hour would be shadowed with the horrors of their daughter's last hour on earth.

Three of the animals had already died. A fourth would now be suffering a horror equal to the Kahls'.

It was two thirty-three A.M.

Hawker still had a reputation to build. And he had plenty of time before daylight.

Hawker made one circle through the Latin district of Starnsdale.

On two different corners a dozen or more young men stood joking and smoking.

They wore red bandannas tied over their heads, like pirates. On the backs of their leather jackets, SATANÁS was sewn in red silk.

Several of them wore chains over their shoulders, like military braid. Others held heavy walking canes in their hands.

In the middle of the block, Hawker noticed, was an abandoned store with bars in the windows. Through the bars Hawker could see more Satanás gang members sitting inside, laughing and drinking.

The men inside looked older. Late twenties, early thirties.

Hawker turned at the end of the block, formulating his plan and, more important, his escape.

Once again he parked near the Hillsboro section. He strapped on a quick-draw shoulder holster over his bare chest, then inserted the .45 Colt Commander he had had customized by the Devel Corporation of Cleveland. They had flared the magazine well, added a Swenson ambidextrous speed safety and an adjustable Bo-Mar rear sight.

Hawker filled three magazines with seven rounds each, fixed one in the Commander, then slid a round in the chamber before adding an eighth round.

He buttoned on a blue, baggy shirt over the weapon.

From the trunk of the car Hawker removed a plastic bottle with a squeeze spout. It contained a thick black liquid.

Hawker stuck a couple more things into his baggy pockets, folded a small grappling hook and forty feet of line through his belt, then locked the car and headed for the Latin section.

He wanted to introduce himself to the Satanás.

An alley connected the backs of buildings on Ybor Avenue. It was used for deliveries and garbage pickups.

Hawker cut down the alley behind the block where the Satanás had collected. It was dank and dark, and it stank of vegetable rot.

Where the alley opened onto a side street, Hawker turned north. The backs of the Satanás gang members were dim shapes in the distance. He could see the glow of their cigarettes.

Hawker pulled his watch cap lower on his head and hugged the shadows. He moved slowly, easily, as if he belonged there. No one saw him. Soon he was close enough to hear the talking.

Hawker stood in the doorway of a tenement building, listening.

They spoke in a fast combination of Spanish and English. Hawker understood enough to know they were talking about a robbery they'd just pulled off. Something funny had happened during the robbery. Their leader, a guy called Magnum, had cut his victim's stomach open, then slipped and fallen in the mess.

It was a perverted version of the old banana peel pratfall, and the Satanás thought it was funny as hell.

As they laughed, Hawker moved behind them. He stopped about forty yards down Ybor Avenue in front of the gang's headquarters. There were groups of gang members at each end of the block, and he could feel them watching him.

Through the dirty windows of the building he could see a half-dozen Hispanic men inside. The floor was covered with trash. One man saw Hawker through the window. Everyone stopped talking.

Hawker smiled at them and winked.

He took the bottle of liquid from his pocket and uncapped it. He held it between his legs and, using his left hand to squeeze the bottle, squirted a wet design on the white stucco wall of the building. He knew it was too dark for them to see the bottle.

"Hey! Hey, motherfucker!" a voice yelled from the street corner. "What you think you doing, man!"

Hawker lifted his head and grinned. All the while he was hurrying to finish the design. "I think I'm pissing on your headquarters—*man*."

The punks had been too shocked to move at first. But now they were trotting toward him. Inside the building the men had drawn handguns.

"Who the fuck you think you are!" another voice yelled.

Hawker jammed the bottle back in his pocket and took out a small AN-MB HC deteriorating smoke grenade. He popped the cardboard canister open and yelled through the screen of copper smoke, "I'll tell you who I am! I . . . am . . . *Satanás!*"

It was a word they would know well. It was the name they had chosen for their gang.

It was also the Spanish word for Satan.

Hawker ran through the smoke toward the next alleyway. They spotted him just as he rounded the corner.

There was a sudden vacuum *whomp*ing impact over his head, and cement exploded at his feet.

They were firing at him.

Hawker ran halfway down the alley. The buildings were only two stories high here, and there were no fire escapes. He took the line and grappling hook from his belt and got it wedged between a brick chimney and the roof on the third throw.

"There's the son of a bitch! Get him!"

A dozen of the Satanás were running at him from the mouth of the alley. Their handguns spurted fire, and slugs whacked into the brick walls beside him, screaming as they ricocheted.

Hawker drew the Colt Commander, steadying it in two big hands. Squatting slightly, he squeezed off three careful rounds.

The punk at the head of the pack exploded backward as if he had been garroted. His gun went spinning.

A second gang member tumbled to the asphalt as a .45 slug destroyed his right thigh.

A third jolted as if he had been hit in midstride by an NFL linebacker. The Commander had busted his shoulder open.

None of them was dead. Hawker didn't want them dead. Not yet.

The others turned tail and ran—but not before Hawker had exploded another smoke grenade and disappeared, so it seemed, into thin air.

On top of the building now, Hawker folded the grappling line and stuffed it back into his belt.

He watched the remaining Satanás trot across the street toward the safety of their headquarters.

They glanced backward over their shoulders, as if they feared being followed.

Hawker could hear them plainly.

"Who the fuck was that guy, cuz?"

"Goddamn if I know, man."

"Said he was the fuckin' devil! Shit!"

"The way he busted heads and disappeared, I 'bout believe it."

"Did you see that shit, cuz? Pweff! Bunch of smoke, and the motherfucker was *gone*."

"Bad dude, man, bad dude. We gotta call an ambulance or something."

"You call the ambulance, cuz. I'm gettin' the hell outta here!"

Hawker took the electronic detonator from his pocket.

The liquid he had squirted on the side of the building was Astrolite. Manufactured by the Explosives Corporation of America, it was still being used experimentally by the United States Army as a replacement for land mines. It could be detected neither visually nor electronically.

Hawker waited until they were thirty yards from their headquarters, then flipped the toggle switch.

He hadn't used much Astrolite, but it achieved the proper effect. The explosion knocked them backward—from fear more than anything.

The wall of their headquarters was engulfed in smoke and fire.

As the smoke dissipated, the design Hawker had created was plain to see.

A couple of the punks knelt in fear, crossing themselves.

"The motherfucker pisses fire, man!"

The others scattered, terrified.

On the wall of their headquarters, in searing white flames, was the outline of a hawk. . . .

four

Hawker awoke just after dawn. He tried to go back to sleep but couldn't.

He got up, made hot tea, and went out to the porch.

The house Jacob Hayes had leased for him was a neat bungalow of redwood and cedar, built on low stilts. Beyond the beach the Pacific Ocean spread away toward the horizon, lifting and rolling in glassy turquoise swells.

The house was in a secluded area of craggy volcanic rock and palms. A hundred yards down the coast a few surfers were out catching the early breakers. Hawker watched them ride the sea, like bright leaves on a green wind.

Farther down the beach high-rises shimmered through the damp sea breeze. Lines of thick copse marked the property boundaries of the bungalow, and Hawker suspected he was living between two beachside mansions.

He finished his tea and stopped at the telephone. He picked it up, then put it down just as quickly. He wanted to call Virgil Kahl. But on the off chance the Kahls might have found a way to sleep after their night of hell, Hawker decided to try later.

He pulled on his Nikes and a pair of running shorts and jogged off down the beach.

Hawker started slow with a long smooth gait, then picked up speed until he was running at about a seven-minute-mile pace. Sand crunched beneath his feet. Sea gulls whirled above, chiding. He passed a few other joggers: a man in an expensive warmup suit and Italian sunglasses; a striking brunette in a tiny bikini top that strained to contain her improbably large breasts.

Neither of them smiled or waved.

Hawker ran about two miles down the beach. The sweat was pouring nicely, matting the copper-colored hair on his chest. He turned and ran back.

Not far from his bungalow he overtook a stunning blonde who jogged calf-deep through the surf. Her neck-length hair was tied back with a blue wind ribbon. The compact weight of her breasts moved in rhythm with the long mahogany legs, and she carried her arms just right, elbows pumping, thighs driving as she seemed to glide through the water.

It took Hawker only a moment to assess her as

one of the rare mixtures: a fine woman athlete
who also happened to be quite beautiful.

Her running was more like a purposeful dance,
and Hawker fought away the urge to slow—or just
stop—and watch her for a while.

He sped on past, noticing that she turned her
head away so she would not have to make eye
contact with him.

Nice people in Los Angeles, Hawker thought.
Real friendly folks.

He began to pick up his own pace, determined
to sprint the last two hundred yards to his cottage.

But the scream stopped him: a surprised female
whoop followed by a painful string of profanities.

Hawker skidded to a halt and saw that the blonde
had fallen. She managed to get her legs under her
again, then hobbled toward the beach, a torn expression on her face. She looked as though she
was in agony.

Hawker ran to her, got her arms around his
neck, and helped the woman to the beach, where
she sat down heavily.

"Ah, *damn*, that hurts," she said, half-crying.
She was massaging the bottom of her right foot.
She wore no shoes.

"Did you sprain your ankle or—"

"No . . . *Christ* . . . something stung me. It
was like being electrocuted."

Firmly, Hawker forced the woman's hands away
so he could see. There was a black puncture hole
in the pad of her foot. The flesh around it was red,
already beginning to swell.

"Do you have stingrays around here?"

The blonde had her eyes squinched tight, her head thrown back. The face was as beautiful as the rest of her. There was something very familiar about the face, but Hawker couldn't place her. "Stingrays?" She grimaced. "*Shit*, I don't know."

"I think you do. I think you just got stung."

Her eyes flashed open: a bright watercolor blue. "Goddamn, I'm not gonna die, am I?" The alarm on her face was real.

Hawker tried not to smile. "I don't think so. You just need something for the pain." He stood and gauged the distance to his cottage, then scooped her up in his arms. She smelled of a nice mixture of shampoo and fresh sweat.

"Hey, are you a doctor or something?"

"Nope."

"Then, maybe you just ought to call an ambulance—"

"We'll get the pain stopped, and then I'll call anybody you want."

Hawker carried her across the beach and up the steps to his cottage. He shoveled her down on one of the plush couches and propped a pillow under her foot.

"Still hurts?"

"It's throbbing like a son of a bitch," she said between clenched teeth.

Hawker hurried into the kitchen and began to rummage through cupboards. The place had been completely stocked, and Hawker knew it had to be there somewhere. He finally found what he

was looking for, pried the lid off, and went back
to the living room.

"Meat tenderizer?" the woman asked incredu-
lously.

"Yep," said Hawker, as he plastered the white
crystals over the stingray wound.

"Where'd you get this cure, buddy—the *National
Enquirer*?" She had been wiggling her foot away
in pain, but she soon stopped. Her eyes grew
wide. "Hey—it's working! No kidding." She flexed
her foot experimentally. "Hell, the pain's almost
completely gone already." She beamed at him as
he returned to the kitchen.

Chuckling, Hawker drew a bucket of warm water.
He emptied the rest of the meat tenderizer into it
and placed the woman's foot in the bucket.

"Let it soak for a few minutes. And it probably
wouldn't hurt to give your doctor a call later. You
want something to drink?"

"Sure. Beer, if you have it."

Hawker went to the refrigerator. On the bottom
rack were rows of Guinness and Tuborg in bottles.
Jacob Montgomery Hayes took good care of him.
He cracked open a bottle of Tuborg and checked
his watch.

It was eight twenty.

He uncapped another bottle for himself and
carried them into the living room. She was loung-
ing back on the couch, her foot thrust out into the
pail. She had high, Germanic cheeks, a delicate
nose and chin, and quick, intelligent eyes. The
blue wind-band made her eyes seem even bluer.

At first glance she looked to be in her mid-twenties. But the roughened skin on the backs of her hands and the cobweb lines at the edge of her eyes told Hawker his first impression was wrong. She had to be in her early or middle thirties.

It didn't detract from the beauty of her. She had the body of an eighteen-year-old.

Hawker handed her the beer, and she downed part of it in long, shameless gulps.

"Ah . . . that's better." She smiled, her eyes dreamy. Hawker studied her closely. He couldn't shake the impression that he had seen her somewhere before. Then it dawned on him: the movies. Films. She was an actress. Melanie St. John. He had seen her in a major role opposite Gene Hackman, and in a smaller part with Robert Redford.

In both films she had played the reserved but sturdy country beauty. Clean of mind, clean of body. She was a lot prettier—and seemed a lot smaller—in real life.

Her language was more interesting, too.

"Soak as long as you want," Hawker said. "I'm going to finish my workout. And in case I don't see you again"—Hawker held out his hand, which she shook absently—"it's been nice meeting you."

"Hey!" she called after him. Hawker stopped in the open door. "You're not leaving already, are you?" She seemed to check herself in midsentence, as if wondering why she would be inquiring into the plans of a stranger. "I mean"—she hesitated—"I don't even know your name. And I haven't even thanked you."

"Hawker. James Hawker. No thanks are necessary. Just pull the door tight when you leave."

Hawker returned to the beach.

The sun was higher and hotter now. A sea breeze battled the smog, and the sky was as pale as Melanie St. John's eyes.

Hawker pulled his shoes off and set his Seiko Submariner watch. He decided to swim for thirty minutes. Fifteen minutes straight out, toward Hawaii. Fifteen minutes back.

He fought his way through the first set of waves, shouldering through them like a linebacker. He began to swim.

At no time in his life could he think more clearly than when he was swimming or running— unless it was in the middle of a fire fight.

The water was cold. It lifted and rolled, so he was either battling his way uphill or sliding down the backside of a wave.

By the time he made it back to the beach, he felt spent but fresh. He fell back-first on the sand, his feet still in the water. He crossed his arms over his eyes to keep out the sun.

"Quite a demonstration," a woman's voice said.

Hawker opened his eyes without moving. Melanie St. John stood over him.

"You should be home resting that foot."

"I thought you said you weren't a doctor." Her laughter was woodwindlike. "I'm wearing a pair of your shoes. My name's Melanie, by the way. I figure anyone who lets me use his shoes deserves to know my first name."

Hawker smiled and said nothing. He had long ago cultivated a private disinterest in public women. Politicians, singers, and actresses—their worlds seem to require them to be self-conscious beyond endurance. Worse, it made them damn boring dates.

Even so, there was something about this woman Hawker liked. She sat down in the sand beside him. Hawker could see the firm curve of her right thigh and calf, and he could see that she was wearing his wornout pair of Nikes.

"You're not from around here, are you?"

Hawker opened his eyes again. "That obvious, huh?"

"Yeah—and you should be glad. The tipoff was that you didn't ask me what I'm *into* or what my horoscope sign is, or where my head is at, or if I'm working on any 'projects' right now. Everything in L.A., by the way, is a project or a property. Also, you haven't used the expressions 'wow' or 'rad'—as in radical—even once."

"Wow," said Hawker. "Imagine that."

She laughed. "The only thing you've done even remotely like a man from L.A. is not make an immediate pass at me."

"California men don't make passes?"

"The gay ones don't. And sometimes it seems like ninety percent of them are gay." She underlined the implied question by adding, "Not that I

disapprove in a moral sense; I don't go around
trying to offend—"

"Sometimes I'm gay," said Hawker.

"Oh . . . oh?"

"Gay—as in pleasantly trouble-free. The other
kind of gay doesn't interest me." He opened his
eyes and winked at her. "How about you?"

"Straight as Old Glory's stripes," she said
theatrically.

"Is that why they're always giving you those
all-American girl parts?"

"You *have* seen my films." She laughed. "I'm
just getting well known enough to pretend I don't
like being recognized, and then you come along
and treat me like a teen-ager with braces. It was
quite a blow to my ego. I was determined to
follow you around until I made you realize—subtly,
of course—that I am a damn famous actress. Did
you know there are no hammers in that bungalow
of yours? I looked."

"Hey, I fixed your foot, didn't I?"

"And an amazing cure it was, too." She stood,
brushing sand from her shorts, then tested her
right leg experimentally. "Almost good as new.
Where'd you learn that meat tenderizer trick?"

"I spent some time in Florida this winter.
They've got more stingrays there than mobile
homes—and that's saying something."

"What are you, a professional beach bum?"

"With a piddling tan like this?"

"I'm surprised you tan at all with that copper-

colored hair of yours. Anyway . . . James? Or is it
Mr. Hawker?"

"My father was Mr. Hawker. I'm anything you
want to call me."

"Hawk, then. That fits you: sort of sleek and
stern. Hey—you're not interested in becoming an
actor, are you? Or maybe you already—"

"Don't worry." He laughed. "I'm not going to
ask you to introduce me to your producer friends.
One of my few talents is knowing what I do or
don't want to do. And I don't want to be an actor."

She seemed relieved, continuing, "Anyway,
Hawk, I want to thank you for helping this morning.
I'm having a few friends over tonight. You know, a
little party. I'll have some food and maybe even a
beer or two. . . . How about stopping by?"

"I may have an appointment. I'm not sure."

She thrust her hands on her hips. "As a famous
actress, I'm not used to being brushed off," she
said with mock severity.

Hawker sat up, grinning. "What time?"

"Oh, ten maybe. Or later. Parties start late in
L.A."

"If I can, I'll be there."

"Great!" she called, already limping away. "That's
my place on the left, right beside yours." She
motioned toward a redwood, multilevel mansion
hidden behind trees. "Getting lost on the way will
be considered a really shitty excuse!"

five

Hawker ate three apples for lunch and drank a quart of water. Finally, he summoned enough courage to call Virgil Kahl. The phone rang nine times, and Hawker was just about to hang up when Kahl answered.

His voice sounded infinitely weary.

"I'm glad to hear from you, James, but I'm really not up to talking. Did you listen to the news this morning? Our . . . our daughter was murdered last night." His voice broke slightly, and Kahl struggled to keep control of himself. "Our dear little Julie. Dead. My God, I still can't accept it. . . ."

Hawker listened and said nothing. Any words of comfort, any offer to help, he knew, would only hurt the grieving man more.

"They found her early this morning," Kahl

continued. "Those . . . those *animals* did it! The Panthers! They murdered our poor little girl!"

"Virgil," Hawker said gently, "if you would like to wait a month or so to continue our project, I'll certainly understand. In fact, it might be best if I just left—"

"*No!*" Kahl interrupted. Understandably, he was transforming all of his hurt into anger. "I'm even more determined to stop them now, James. We must! We have to fight these creatures. There comes a time when even civilized people must drop the sham of reason and take up arms. It's time to fight, James, and we need you now more than ever."

"I'll do what I can, Virgil."

"While we . . . we were awaiting word from the police last night, I called all the men on our original neighborhood watch force. I suggested a meeting at one of our members' homes. Eight thirty tonight. I see no reason to call the meeting off. In fact, I think we have even more reason to go ahead with the plans."

"Who should I ask for?"

"A man named John Cranshaw. Oh, and James— don't be surprised if the reception you get from some of the members is a little cool. Some of them didn't like the idea of an outsider coming in to help. Especially watch for a man named Sully McGraw. He can be a—" In the background Kahl was interrupted by a high, wailing cry. "Oh, lord," he said shakily. "My wife's woken up again. She's

gone quite mad, James. . . . I've got to call the
doctor. I'm sorry. . . ."

Hawker jotted down the hasty address Kahl
gave him and hung up, feeling both sorrow and
frustration.

He needed information. He had to find a way to
go to the very source of the gangs, find out who or
what motivated them, and for what purpose.

He couldn't just go on killing the punks one by
one.

But for the time being it was the only plan of
attack he had.

And until something better came along, it would
have to do. . . .

Just after seven Hawker slid into his rented
Cutlass and drove down Highland Avenue, parallel
to the beach.

The sun was evaporating westward, toward Japan.

More surfers were out, the pretty surfing group-
ies trotting heavy-breasted down the beach, their
nylon bikinis the color of psychedelic Easter eggs.

Hawker had never seen a heavier concentration
of beautiful girls in his life. Driving through early-
Saturday-night traffic, he decided it must be because, during the nineteen thirties and forties, every
good-looking, out-of-work man and woman in the
country probably gravitated to Hollywood, dream-
ing of stardom.

Few of them made it, of course.

Those who didn't probably settled for menial
jobs. And dull marriages.

But they certainly had produced some beautiful babies.

Hawker stopped at a Greek restaurant, ate two gyros with extra sauce, and bought the afternoon paper.

In a city festering with crime Julie Kahl hadn't been given much space. It was at the bottom of the local section—two paragraphs on the front, and then the story jumped to an inside page.

Considering Julie's death the reporter hammered at the gory details—multiple rape, mutilation with a knife, the naked corpse, et cetera.

Hawker hoped like hell Virgil Kahl or his wife didn't read the story.

Only two paragraphs interested Hawker:

> *Arrested at the scene was Martin "Cat Man" Washington. Washington was charged with rape, one count of first-degree murder, and three counts of second-degree murder, as well as possession of an illegal automatic weapon.*
>
> *Police speculate that the four members of the notorious "Panthers" street gang began to fight among themselves after the rape-murder of Ms. Kahl. Washington, with seventeen prior arrests on his record, was also seriously wounded. He is listed in critical but stable condition at Dominguez Hills Hospital.*

John Cranshaw's home was two blocks from the Kahl residence, and twice as large.

A stucco wall screened it from the street. Hawker

noted the bottle shards cemented into the top of the wall to keep out burglars—an old and unfriendly Mexican custom.

There were so many cars parked along the curb, it looked as though the Cranshaws were having a party.

Instead it was more like a wake. Or a funeral.

About twenty men sat on folding chairs outside. Two thick almond trees sheltered them from the gathering dusk of the summer night.

There was no laughter, no loud and friendly conversation.

The men sat with their hands folded, heads slightly bent as if expecting a blow. They spoke in low voices, as if in a church.

A squat, heavyset man with a white beard approached Hawker. "James Hawker? Good, we've been expecting you. I'm John Cranshaw. Come sit beside me at the front of the group. I'll introduce you."

Cranshaw had a pallid complexion but a good handshake. His mustache and his fingers were stained yellow with nicotine. Even as he introduced himself to Hawker, he mechanically lit another cigarette, hacking as he inhaled.

As Cranshaw opened the meeting, Hawker took a careful visual survey of the men before him.

Most of them were between thirty and fifty years old. The majority of them were white, with a few blacks and Latins sprinkled among them.

Physically they were not an intimidating bunch.

But they didn't have to be. Hawker had learned

early during his career as a cop that physical speed and strength don't count for much on the street. Not when compared to the efficiency of a well-organized group, a group led by a man—or men—who refused to back down.

A team with courage and leadership would win every single time.

Now all he had to do was convince this group.

One man in the group caught his attention. He was a huge, red-faced man with jet-black hair combed straight back. He had to weigh close to three hundred pounds. His metal chair bowed beneath him as if it were made of rubber.

But what particularly set him apart was the furious scowl on his face, and the way he kept slapping his fist into his palm. Hawker wondered if he might be the man Virgil Kahl had warned him about—Scully McGraw. Even if he wasn't, Hawker decided, he'd bear watching.

Cranshaw went over what the watch members could do for the Kahls, and the date of Julie Kahl's funeral. Wisely, he pointed out that people from their ranks had been murdered before—and that it might happen again.

When it was Hawker's turn to speak, he told them of the success of other such groups. He outlined how he could help them improve their own methods—as long as they were willing to train. He spoke slowly and carefully, taking care not to insult them by mentioning their past failures. He finished by saying they should talk privately among themselves. If they wanted his help, it was available.

He was about to sit down when the huge man with the black hair stood.

"I want to ask you something, Hawker," he snapped. "Just who in the fuck do you think you are coming in here from God-knows-where, telling us how to run our program? The daughter of one of our members was raped last night by a bunch of niggers, and you come here telling us we should fall in line like Boy Scouts."

Hawker noticed the black men in the group flinch and tighten as the man spoke.

A couple of other men yelled, "Sit down, Scully. The guy's just trying to help."

"What about it, Hawker?" Scully demanded. "Personally, I think you're just a little pile of shit who likes to act important. Now, if any man in here has the balls to join me, I'll take him with me into the streets to crack a head or two."

Scully had been gradually moving closer and closer to Hawker, heading for the gate out. As he brushed near, Hawker held out his arm, stopping him. He could feel the eyes of every man in the place on him.

"You know something?" Hawker asked easily.

"No. So, tell me, asshole." Scully had whirled to face him.

"I'm having a hard time deciding whether you're obnoxious or just plain hungry," Hawker went on. "I know how mean fat people can get when they're hungry."

Scully's slab of face turned red as the other men laughed.

He made a bellowing sound and swung a bearlike right fist at Hawker. Hawker saw it coming and ducked under it. Turning sideways, he slammed his elbow into Scully's soft solar plexus. The air whooshed out of the fat man, bending him over.

Hawker cocked his hips and jolted Scully's head back with a right uppercut that crossed the man's eyes and sent him teetering mountainously. The other men seemed to tense themselves for the resulting crash.

It never came. Hawker caught the man by the collar and lowered him gently to the ground.

He looked at the others and shrugged. "I'm sorry, fellows. I had no choice."

He loosened Scully McGraw's collar and checked his pulse. The heart was pounding away like a hammer in the huge chest.

Hawker stood and nodded to them. "Think my offer over, gentlemen. Remember, there's no reason in the world why anyone in this country should have to live in fear. Together, we can put a stop to it."

Hawker thanked John Cranshaw, then walked outside alone.

six

Hawker considered making another assault on the street gangs but decided against it for two reasons.

There would be a lot of police activity after Julie Kahl's murder, and Hawker had no desire to end up running from the local cops.

The second reason was that he felt he deserved a break. Melanie St. John's party was a little too tempting to pass up.

Hawker wasn't wild about parties. And he didn't relish the idea of listening to a bunch of actors he had never met rattle on about their work.

But he did like the idea of seeing the stunning Melanie St. John again.

Hopefully it would be worth an uncomfortable evening of loud music, loud talk, and manufactured smiles.

He drove back to his beachside cottage. The

sun had left a pale orange haze on the western horizon, like rust. Stars glimmered. The wind tapped at the chimes on the porch of his bungalow.

Hawker stripped to his shorts and opened a cold beer. He put ice in a bucket and jammed his swollen right hand in. Punching people is not good for the knuckles. He sat on the porch drinking the good beer, his hand in the bucket, watching the night surf roll in.

When he could bear the aching cold no longer, he went inside and soaped himself warm in the shower. He scrubbed his hair clean, lathered and shaved, then padded barefoot to the bedroom.

Hawker always traveled light—one canvas carry-on that would slide under a plane seat—so he chose his clothes carefully. The clothes had to meet three requirements: they had to be comfortable; they had to be practical; and they had to be honest enough in design so that they wouldn't make him stand out in a crowd.

Hawker liked his anonymity. And that meant looking neither like a slob nor an *Esquire* fashion mannequin.

He chose a pair of soft summer lamb's-wool socks and then pulled himself into a pair of white military twill slacks. The pocket pleats and adjustable waistband were standard on RAF-issue pants during the war. It didn't take him long to decide not to wear a tie, so he pulled a lime-colored cotton mesh shirt over his head before brushing his short, copper hair into place.

After slipping into a pair of glove-soft Timberland deck shoes, he was ready. He cracked another bottle of Tuborg and headed outside.

It was ten twenty-five.

Melanie St. John's "little" party consisted of about a hundred people drinking and dancing and talking—all at the same time.

The house was huge, built high into the trees, and the circular drive was jammed with Rolls-Royces, Mercedes, and Jags. A couple of teen-age boys, working as parking valets, sat outside smoking a joint. They didn't even look up as Hawker walked past.

Inside, an electric band pounded out some esoteric acid-rock classic. It sounded like one long car wreck. There was a door bell, but it would have been ridiculous to use it.

Hawker swung open the double doors and went in.

The house was a back-to-basics marvel: huge, raw wood-beam ceiling, a stone fireplace, Navajo weaves hanging from the open balcony which spread across one whole upper side of the house.

People danced on the balcony, near the fireplace, and directly in front of the band. They danced and shouted and mingled, shoulder to elbow.

The place was packed with people, and all the people—so it seemed to Hawker—looked as if they came straight from a fashion magazine, or else straight from the silver screen.

Hawker recognized a few of the faces. Major rock stars. A few major film stars, and a lot of lesser knowns.

The women all wore dresses styled so that their breasts were on ready display with any twist or turn they made.

The men all looked as though they either went to the same hairdresser—or were hairdressers.

Smiling, Hawker worked his way through the crowd to the corner of the house farthest from the band. There was a table of hors d'oeuvres there, and he began to eat.

A tawny-haired starlet in a sheer white dress stood beside him. He recognized her as the actress who played the sterotypical dizzy blonde on a current situation comedy. Supposedly, she had done for the T-shirt what Marilyn Monroe had done for the sweater.

The white dress was transparent where her breasts strained against the sheer material.

She looked at Hawker, then looked at him again. She snapped her fingers, saying, "Leo, right?"

"Leo? No. My name is—"

"Not your name, silly." The woman giggled. She had the same high-pitched voice she used on television, and Hawker realized she probably was very much like the character she portrayed. "Leo— like the sign. Your moon sign."

"Oh." Hawker couldn't remember what sign he was. "Yeah. Leo—right. I'm a Leo." All he could remember was that he *wasn't* a Leo.

She clasped her hands together, pleased with herself. "I just knew it. I can always tell a Leo man. People always sort of move out of the way when a Leo man walks into the room. They're very masterful, you know."

"They are?"

"*You* are, silly."

She smiled at him. "My name's Trixie McCall."

"And I'm—"

"No, no," she insisted. "Let me guess. I guessed your sign, and I bet I can guess your name, too. I'm a moon child, and moon children have well-developed psychic powers. Even my astrologer says so." She put her hand against her forehead, as if trying to communicate with the dead.

Hawker waited, feeling foolish. He felt as if he were talking to a twelve-year-old who had taken an overdose of hormone pills. Across the room Melanie St. John caught his eye with a wave of her hand. She began to elbow her way toward him.

Trixie McCall's face brightened. "Doug! You're name is Doug, isn't it!"

"Doug it is," said Hawker agreeably.

Trixie shook herself, delighted. She slipped her arm through his, resting the heat of her left breast on his bicep. "I get a good feeling from you, Doug."

"And I'm getting a nice feeling from you, too, Trixie."

She cuddled closer. "Don't you think these parties are kinda silly? Out in the car I've got a couple of nice grams we could sniff. Then maybe we could slip into the Jacuzzi downstairs before it gets too crowded."

"Crowded?"

"Oh, I don't mind a few people watching, but I don't want a whole audience. I'm kind of a prude that way."

"Why, James Hawker—as I live and breathe," interrupted Melanie St. John, thrusting out her hand as if she were one New England farmer meeting another. She wore a slate-blue blouse of satin, and her blond hair was combed boyishly back, as if styled by the wind. She was beautiful.

Hawker untangled himself and took Melanie's hand, rolling his eyes.

"His name is *Doug*," Trixie McCall pouted.

"I'm a Leo," offered Hawker.

"And he's with me," said Trixie, glaring like a cat about to fight for its prey.

"There, there," said Melanie, as if soothing a child. "You'll find someone else to play with, Trixie. This man's a doctor. He needs his rest." Melanie slipped her arm through Hawker's and led him away.

"I knew you were a doctor!" Trixie McCall called after them. "I could *sense* it!"

Melanie made her way through the crowd, smiling and nodding, fending off conversation. Outside they walked down the steps and across the lawn to the beach.

The air seemed fresher after the smoke and noise of the party. The surf rolled through the darkness, crashing on the reef.

"Hope I didn't spoil your plans for the evening," she chided.

"I couldn't tell if Trixie wanted me for dessert or the main course."

"She does have a healthy appetite, and strictly carnivorous." She turned to him. "If you want to go with her, I certainly won't—"

"I'm funny about women," Hawker cut in. "They have to be reasonably intelligent, or they leave me cold."

"My, don't we have high standards?"

"Reasonably intelligent means being able to spell 'tree.' I think Trixie would have had a tough time."

"So you were really about to turn down America's hottest new sex symbol?" She gave him a look of appraisal. "Damn—I think you would have."

"Don't be too impressed. The night's young. My standards shrink in direct proportion to the amount of beer I've had. Even so, I began to lose interest in Trixie when she suggested we go out for a little snort of cocaine."

Melanie St. John was no longer smiling. "You don't approve?"

"No, I don't. I don't approve one little bit. I'm too much in awe of the human brain to think we should drug it for recreation. As far as other people go, I think anyone has the right to do to themselves what they damn well please. There are all kinds of ways to commit suicide, and it's a free country. But when someone begins to sell, or give, or even offer their brand of suicide to someone else, that's when it becomes a criminal act. And I think it's wrong."

As he spoke, her head lowered and then she turned away from him.

"I'm sorry if I offended you, Melanie," he said. "It's your house and your party, but I've got a bad habit of saying what I think. I'll leave if you like."

"No," she said softly. "Don't leave. Stay." She reached out and took his arm, and they began to walk back toward the house. They walked for a time in silence. She said, finally, "Drugs are a way of life out here, Hawk. And if you spend any time in L.A., you'll learn it's true. God knows, I did. I got my first film part seven years ago. I was twenty-three and a little naive. People offered me drugs, so I took them. Everybody was doing it. I thought it was a requirement for stardom, or some damn silly thing like that. I got more and more involved. I made a bad marriage. I'd like to blame it all on drugs, but I can't. I was a bitch of a wife, and my husband was the star of a smash TV series who spent more time looking in the mirror than I did."

Hawker stopped walking. "There's no need for you to tell me this, Melanie."

"I want to," she said. "You're a stranger, and somehow it's easier to talk to a stranger. The right stranger, anyway." She squeezed his arm briefly. "Why is it I feel like I can trust you, Hawk?"

"It's called 'transference.' A doctor-patient phenomenon. It happens every time I fix someone's foot."

She chuckled softly. "Anyway, the marriage broke up. And I started using drugs more and more heavily. Last year I got involved with"—she hesitated—"I got involved with another actor. He lived for drugs. I think it's a business with him.

"Anyway, I moved in with this guy. He has a place at Malibu. From what I remember, every day was a party. He has a lot of friends who aren't in the business. Rough-looking guys. They loved it. They feast on starlets. People on the outside don't realize it, Hawk, but Hollywood—meaning the film world—is a nasty, nasty place. There are a lot of sickos around. Fanatics. They hang around the outskirts of the business like sharks. Charles Manson types. You never know when these freaks are going to bust into your place and start shooting people, or cutting people. They take strange drugs, and they join even stranger cults. For some weird reason this guy I was living with courted these types. He said they were 'interesting studies.' You know, that 'actors are really artists who must study' bullshit."

"So what happened?"

She stopped in the darkness of the driveway. From the house came the sound of wild laughter and the driving electric rhythm of the band. She shrugged. "One night we had a party at his place. A friend of mine, an actress who was into drugs not even as heavily as I was, came. I found her the next morning. She was outside, stark naked. Three or four of my boyfriend's sicko friends were taking turns on her. She was drugged out. Didn't even know what was happening. My boyfriend kept a gun, and I ran the sickos off. My girl friend didn't wake up for another hour. And you know what the first thing she said was? She said, 'Hey, great party, Melanie.' The poor thing didn't even know what had happened to her.

"That was eight weeks ago, Hawk. That's when it finally dawned on me; that's when I realized what I had become. I moved back into my place that day. Didn't even tell my boyfriend I was going. All that night I stayed up ranting and raving like a madwoman. The next night was tough, too—but not as tough. I told myself I'd stay clean or die. And I stayed clean, because I knew it was true. I *would* have died, sooner or later.

"I gave it all up: drugs, alcohol, even cigarettes. And you know what? For the first time in many, many years I feel good. I really *like* myself. I get up at dawn and go for my run. I work hard all day, and then I come home and run again. I think the poison is finally gone from my system, but it took a hell of a lot of sweating to do it." She chuckled and motioned toward the house. "This party is like an official release from my own private clinic."

"A celebration?"

"No. I think I had to prove to myself that I could suffer through a party without taking a drink or sniffing some coke. So I decided to throw a test party—and invite the wildest partygoers I knew."

"You're not even tempted a little bit?"

"That's the weird thing—I expected to be, but I'm not. Those people in there used to be my world. Now they're like strangers. Just silly, spoiled kids who can't grow up; adult kids who have to play their game of 'the tortured artist' or 'life in the fast lane' because they think that is what's expected. The games used to be important to me. Now they just seem tragic."

Her arms were folded across her chest, and she was looking out toward the Pacific. Her eyes glistened. Hawker put his hand on her shoulder, and she leaned against him, her head on his chest. "Thank you," he said gently. "I don't know why you told me, but I'm glad you did."

She sniffed and wiped her nose comically. "Maybe it's because you're the only one square enough around here to appreciate it."

"Hah! Square, am I?"

She stood on her tiptoes, kissed him quickly on the mouth, and took his hand. "Anyone not in the movie business is square, buster." She pulled at him, grinning. "Help make a tour of my health spa, and I'll prove it to you."

"You have a health spa?"

"Hell, yes. My manager says I'm rich, so why not? Come on."

Hawker followed her around the house and through a tall redwood gate. There was a tennis court, lighted. The light spilled over into the lime-green swimming pool. About a dozen men and women swam naked. They shouted and laughed, treading water to keep their drinks safe. Someone switched the underwater lights on, and they laughed louder.

Another group of people hunched intently over a table. Four neat lines of white powder had been separated on the glass top. Trixie McCall sat at the table. She had stripped off her dress and now wore only sheer bikini panties. Her hair was wet, and water glistened on the famous breasts.

Concentrating mightily, she rolled a bill into a tight tube. Hawker noted that it was a twenty-dollar bill. He turned away before she used the bill to pipe the cocaine up her nose.

Beyond the pool was a full bar. Beside the bar was a massive Jacuzzi whirlpool bath.

The lights were on in the Jacuzzi, and Hawker watched a muscular blond-haired man and a black woman, both aroused and glassy-eyed, locked in pounding intercourse.

The man seemed to take strange pleasure in stopping just as the woman was at her climactic peak. He made a show of stopping to reposition her, plainly enjoying the chance to exhibit his freakish size.

Other men and women, chest-deep in water beside them, watched idly.

Melanie wrapped her arm around Hawker's waist. Her voice seemed small and far away. "How about it, James? Are you square or not?"

Hawker made a confused motion with his arms. "Where's the weird stuff you wanted to show me? This is just a typical Saturday night back in Illinois."

She laughed, relieved. "Thanks for not being shocked. Anyway, this is the last big party I'll ever have. And I'm already anxious for them to leave. So how about doing a lady a favor. How about sitting with me out on the beach until a reasonable time rolls around and I can tell them all to get the hell out." She grinned at him, her blue eyes crisp and clear. "You can tell me your life story, okay?"

Hawker didn't get a chance to answer.

As he was about to speak, a hand grabbed his shoulder and turned him roughly away. Hawker had no trouble recognizing the man who stood before him.

It was Johnny Barberino. Hawker had never seen any of his movies, but he had seen the advertisements. Barberino had started out as a teen-ager in television dramas and then gone on to become America's heartthrob by doing a series of discotheque rock operas. His screen image consisted of dancing, loving, and fighting.

Hawker had the uncomfortable realization that this was Melanie St. John's unnamed boyfriend.

"I want to talk to you, Melanie," he commanded. He gave Hawker a brief, burning look, then ignored him. "I want to talk to you *now*. Alone."

Hawker felt the woman draw near him, holding his arm. "No, Johnny. I told you I wasn't going to talk anymore, and I told you to stay the hell off my property. Now go, damn it, before I call the police."

Hawker admired the bravery in her voice all the more because of the fear he saw in her eyes.

The pool area was suddenly silent. People were watching and listening.

Hawker got the impression they were hoping for another freak show.

Behind Johnny Barberino his two rough-looking friends stood easily. They wore mild, drugged-out grins on their faces.

"Goddamn it, Melanie, you're going to come with me right now! Either that, or tell all of these schmucks to get the fuck out so we can—"

"They're not going anywhere, Johnny. You are. You're leaving right now. I'm going to call the police."

She turned and stalked off toward the stairs. Hawker saw Barberino's hand spear out to grab her, and he intercepted the actor's hand midway. Squeezing his wrist, Hawker said easily, "Shouldn't grab, now, should we? Why don't you let the lady make her phone call, like a good boy."

"And why don't you fuck off, asshole!" Barberino jerked his hand away. He glanced around, as if to make sure his buddies were behind him. They were.

Hawker had no desire to get involved in a fight with a movie star—and he especially didn't want to be around when the cops came to break it up. He held his palms out, saying, "Look, there's no sense in fighting about this. Why don't you and your friends just take off?"

Barberino took it as a sign of fear. He flashed an evil grin. "Too late to try and talk your way out of it now, fucker!" He held his fists up in the stance of a fighter. It was like a pose for a movie poster. He spoke louder now, so everyone could hear how he was making the red-haired stranger back down. "You give *me* shit, man, and I'll jam it right back down your throat!"

Hawker turned to walk away. A hand grabbed him from behind and swung him around. Barberino threw a series of fast jabs at his head. He was too far away to connect. Hawker didn't even flinch.

"Playing badass, now, huh?" Barberino was bobbing and weaving as he talked. "Why don't you try to turn and run away again, dumb shit?"

"Naw," said Hawker as his hands made slow fists. "You had your chance. I think it's time someone kicked that famous ass of yours."

Barberino shot out another series of jabs—these, too close. Hawker knocked his fist away and ducked under the awkward right cross. He planted his left foot on top of the actor's shoe, then slapped him three quick times in the face, hard.

"Don't you hit my face, you son of a bitch!" Barberino roared, outraged.

He jerked his knee up, but Hawker caught most of it with his hip.

"You have to learn not to give strangers orders, sonny," Hawker said. He buried his left fist in the actor's side, then put his weight behind a right that caught Barberino flush on the side of the neck. He spun around like a top, bent at the hips. Hawker timed it just right. His kick caught the actor in the seat of the pants, driving him into the pool.

"He's got a knife, Doug! Look out!"

Hawker was glad, for once, he had met the dizzy Trixie McCall.

Barberino's two friends had been patiently waiting for the actor to polish off Hawker. Now they had decided it was their job.

They looked more like members of a motorcycle gang than actors. Hawker remembered what Melanie had said about her boyfriend's sick friends.

One thing was for sure. These two were playing for keeps.

They each had knives.

Slowly, they came at Hawker. They were stalking him, knives held low, and vectoring.

Hawker backed away, careful not to stumble.

They were trying to trap him against the fence.

From the corner of his eye he noticed Johnny Barberino crawling groggily out of the pool. He also noticed a beer bottle on a stand by the pool.

Hawker grabbed the bottle. He faked once as if to throw, then really did throw it. He had played two seasons of professional baseball in the Tigers' organization, and he could still throw hard enough to make the ball hop between home and second. The bottle jolted the man's head back like a .45 slug.

He fell to the deck, face bloody, unconscious.

The second man lunged at Hawker. The knife blade razored through Hawker's shirt as he jumped back. Hawker caught the man's arm in both hands and drove it down against his knee.

The elbow joint popped like firewood.

A thin scream escaped the man's lips, but Hawker was no longer in a forgiving mood. He wrapped his fist in the matted black hair and clubbed the man's face to pulp with a series of short rights.

"*Hawk!* Stop! James, please stop. You'll kill him!"

Melanie St. John was pulling him away. Realizing she was right, Hawker shook his hand free.

The man fell in a heap at his feet.

The fury still cold in his gray eyes, Hawker searched the area until he saw Johnny Barberino. The actor was cowering in a corner by the dressing rooms. The right side of his neck was already purple, and swelling. His carefully combed hair hung in a wet mess over his ears. He looked at Hawker, then looked quickly away.

Hawker pointed at him. "Get the hell out of here, you obnoxious little punk," he whispered between clenched teeth. Barberino got to his feet, sulking. Hawker stomped his foot. "Now!"

The actor half-walked and half-trotted toward the gate, yelling over his shoulder, "You'll pay for this, motherfucker. You'll be damn sorry you ever touched me!" Barberino was still yelling threats as he disappeared.

Melanie was working on his shirt. "Christ, they tried to stab you. You're bleeding, Hawk."

By the table Trixie McCall stood, looking at him with concern. Hawker winked and nodded. "Thanks for the help," he called to her. She still wore only the bikini underwear.

Now that she was standing, Hawker could see that her national admiration was well deserved.

Melanie saw what he was looking at. She took him primly by the arm. "This time I'll play doctor," she said, leading him away. "And my first orders are: Take your eyes off little Miss Trixie's scenic peaks."

She pulled herself closer to him, adding in a whisper, "You have other mountains to climb. . . ."

seven

The next night Hawker continued his assault on the street gangs. He waited until first dusk, then headed for Starnsdale's black slums.

He had one objective: terrorism.

If Virgil Kahl was right, fear and violence were the only two things the Panthers would understand.

Hawker was determined to give them plenty of both. People who are frightened lose their confidence. And they make mistakes.

Hawker also knew that frightened people are dangerous. Damn dangerous.

Like rats trapped in a corner, people who are scared will fight to the death.

Even so, he had to soften up the street gangs. He had to make them vulnerable if the citizens of Hillsboro were to have a fighting chance against them.

They needed all the help they could get.

That afternoon Hawker had had his first training session with the Hillsboro watch group. The men in the group, it seemed, were good men. They had homes and kids and businesses.

They had plenty to fight for. But they were not fighters.

Not yet, anyway. They lacked training and they lacked confidence.

One would follow the other, Hawker hoped. Because to fight effectively, he knew, men had to practice. To be successful, they had to work. And work damn hard.

Courage was just another facet of confidence. And confidence could only be built through hard training.

Hawker told the men this. It seemed to cheer them. Hard work was something they could understand. They had all worked hard in their lives. It made the possibility of success seem within their reach. It took that strange word *fighting* out of the frightening, near-mystic world of machismo.

Hard work was something they could all understand, young and old, fat and thin.

The enthusiasm showed on their faces.

Only Sully McGraw was less than enthusiastic. Hawker was surprised he'd even shown up.

Even so, the huge fat man took orders, followed instructions, and kept his mouth shut.

In the spirit of reconciliation Hawker tried to draw him into conversation during one of their

breaks. The file Jacob Hayes had given Hawker
included brief biographies on many of the men in
the watch group. McGraw, a widower, was the
father of three adult daughters. He owned a chain
of Los Angeles hock shops, and he was a member
of several ultra-right-wing citizens' organizations.

Hawker decided business was a safe conversational topic, and he asked him about his hock
shops.

Sully favored him with a long, wilting look and
walked away.

"Real talkative guy," Hawker said to John
Cranshaw, who had witnessed the one-sided
exchange.

"McGraw can be a little strange," Cranshaw
explained. "But he's one of the most imposing
figures in the group. We need him."

Hawker could only agree.

Hawker began with the basics: safe confrontation of a suspect. Proper backup positioning. Hand
signals among team members. Travel overwatch.

It was simple stuff, straight from the SWAT
handbook. Hawker drilled it into the men until he
was sure they had it—then he drilled it in some
more.

He told them they had one simple responsibil-
ity during their training:

"You must learn this stuff so well," he instructed,
"that, when you're in a tight spot, you will do
everything automatically. You won't have time to
think. You won't have time to search your memory.

Your life, or the life of a team member, can depend on how automatically you react."

After two hours of intensive training Hawker turned the group over to Cranshaw for the closing meeting.

He drove back to his bungalow on Manhattan Beach to shower, eat, and maybe even get a little rest before his assault on the Panthers.

He hadn't gotten much sleep at all the previous night. As he drove through the wild Sunday traffic, Hawker couldn't help thinking about Melanie St. John.

After his fight with Johnny Barberino and the two goons, she had walked him back to his cottage. With the efficiency of a trained nurse she had stripped his shirt away and studied the shallow knife scrape across his stomach.

"What's the prognosis, doctor?"

"I think you're very lucky, Hawk."

"You say that with authority. It's not a line from some role you've played, is it? Florence Nightingale?"

"I play the pretty rural type, with a backbone of steel, remember?"

He touched her chin and kissed her softly. "Typecasting."

She returned the kiss, holding his head, her lips soft and swollen. Then she pulled away, exhaling loudly. "Hey, don't get me started."

"Hard for you to stop?"

She eyed him shrewdly. "With you it would be. Besides, I need to get your cut taken care of, then walk back home and say good night to my guests—not to mention the police."

Hawker put his hands behind his head and said nothing. She scrubbed the cut clean, added disinfectant, and bandaged it.

Noticing the scars on his left shoulder, she hesitated, then said, "It looks like you make a habit of this sort of thing."

"I'm accident-prone."

"My, we are evasive, aren't we?" She tore off a strip of surgical tape. "I just realized that you know a good deal about me, but I don't know a single thing about you. Maybe it's the way you listen. You smile at the right places, and nod at the right places, and it gives people the impression you care so much, it's like you're really communicating without talking."

"Oh?"

"Yeah. So talk to me, Hawk. What are you doing in L.A.? What kind of work do you do? Are there a pretty little wife and kids back home? And—"

"And where did I get the scars, right? You're pretty nosy, woman."

Her voice was formal, but the words weren't. "I like you. You're an interesting and attractive male. I'm an unattached female—not that I'm interested in *being* attached—and you are completely different from the men I've known out here. So I want to hear about you." She paused for a moment, then gave him a studied gaze. "For some reason I keep thinking you're a cop."

"I was. In Chicago. I quit less than a year ago."

"And now?"

"Now I'm looking. I saved some money. My ex-wife runs an art gallery that provides her with a penthouse apartment and a Mercedes. She's a very nice and very smart lady who doesn't need my support. We had no kids. I wish we had. So I'm on my own, scars and all."

"That's a pretty simple story."

"I'm a pretty simple guy."

"Are you sure you're not still a cop? Maybe one of the feds, sent out here to Tinseltown to get the real dope—excuse the pun—on us actors?"

"Not me."

"I'm almost disappointed. I was hoping you would at least be a private eye or something."

"Sam Spade at your service."

"I thought your name was Doug."

"Now even I'm getting confused."

They both laughed. The laughter lapsed into a comfortable silence. They barely spoke as Melanie finished up. As she opened the door to leave, she stopped and turned. "When I get finished over there, I may be too tired to move. I'll probably just take a shower and crawl in bed."

"Fine."

"It was nice meeting you, James."

"Nice meeting you, Melanie."

She took a step out the door, then stopped again. She grinned. "You can be a real bastard, you know it? You're not even going to ask me to come back, are you?"

"I guess that ought to be your decision."

She shrugged and smiled. "I guess you're right," she said.

Hawker read for two hours, waiting, then drifted off to sleep. He awoke to the click of the door latch.

She was silhouetted against the gray expanse of the window and the sea outside.

Slowly, as if weaving to music, she stepped out of her slacks and unbuttoned her blouse, turning sideways to the window.

Her breasts were swollen cones, the nipples elongated and pointed upward. She rolled her head back, combing her fingers through her flaxen hair, then ran her hands down the sides of her body. In one fluid motion she stripped off her panties.

"That's quite an entrance," Hawker said softly.

Her laughter was shy. "I didn't know you were awake. You might have said something before I was . . . naked."

"Who could sleep with all that beauty going on?"

She moved across the room and knelt beside the bed. "Hey," she whispered. "I feel like kissing." She touched her soft lips to his, her tongue tracing the corners of his mouth. She drew away and smiled, then kissed him harder, mouth wide, lips searching.

"How about some light petting?"

"Would Dear Abby approve?"

"Let the old dear find her own man."

Melanie's hand searched beneath the covers until she found him with her soft fingers, stroking gently.

Hawker lifted her onto the bed beside him. His hand spread wide, he touched the expanse of her firm stomach, pausing on the abrupt flexure of her right breast.

The flesh was firm beneath his hand, the erect nipple like a heated projectile between his thumb and forefinger.

Melanie St. John moaned, her whole body trembling. "Awww . . . that feels so nice, James . . . *yes* . . . do that; keep doing that. . . ."

Hawker found her breasts with his lips, then followed the curve of her perfect body downward.

"You're my first movie star, lady," he whispered.

She chuckled. "How do you like it so far?"

"I'm already anxious for the reruns. . . ."

So Hawker thought about Melanie St. John as he drove.

And he thought about her as he unlocked the door of his cottage and went inside.

And he thought about her as he opened a tin of hash, and cracked eggs to fry for his supper.

You're as bad as a damn moon-eyed teen-ager, he thought as he ate.

It took a concentrated effort, but he shrugged the fresh memory of the woman away and turned his attention to his plans for the evening.

Jacob Hayes had shipped Hawker's equipment to California in stout wooden crates. After he ate,

Hawker finished opening the crates. The weaponry arsenal was impressive. Hawker hoped he wouldn't have to use it all—because, if he did, it would mean war had begun. All-out war.

Carefully he unloaded his electronic gear. He placed the keyboard of his 128K RAM computer on the desk by the telephone in the guest room. He mounted the video screen on top of the keyboard, then patched in the telephone modem.

He tested the equipment and found it operative.

There were more electronics, and Hawker unpacked it all. The most impressive addition to the hardware was a HFR Eavesdrop, a high-technology listening system built for the U.S. government by IBM.

Hawker unpacked the booster/receiver, which looked like a portable shortwave radio. There was a cassette tape recorder built in. The recorder was sound-sensitive, which meant it would automatically tape any conversation within the area of its minireceivers—little candy-colored bugs. The Eavesdrop's antenna was a modernistic dish, about the size of a suitcase.

In the growing darkness Hawker found a ladder and mounted the antenna dish on top of the bungalow, then ran the coaxial cable inside to the receiver.

He showered, then dressed in dark jeans, black knit pullover shirt, and his black watch-cap.

Hawker selected the weapons he wanted to carry and placed them in the Cutlass. Finally he took a plastic sack containing a dozen of the tiny bugging devices.

After the drinking bouts of Friday and Saturday nights the Starnsdale slums seemed to be in the grip of a massive hangover. The few people who roamed the streets were subdued. The pounding soul music which vibrated from the rows of sour bars wasn't turned up quite so loud.

The stray dogs and the winos slept side by side in the alleyways.

Hawker parked his car near the Hillsboro section, then retraced his route back to the slums.

He made his way across the tops of buildings, staying low, hugging the shadows.

The summer stink of asphalt and garbage lifted from the streets. As Hawker moved over the slum apartments, he could smell the fried-fat-and-greens odor of late suppers cooking.

Not far from where Julie Kahl was murdered, Hawker saw them: about two dozen men and teenagers wearing blue bandannas and sleeveless T-shirts.

They stood in serious conversation on a street corner. There were no jokes and little laughter.

Several of them carried wicked-looking clubs. Others had heavy chains wrapped around their necks like necklaces.

Something was up. Hawker recognized the signs. These guys were looking for a fight.

Hawker decided he would give it to them.

He hid himself behind a chimney, two stories

above them. He crawled on his belly to the edge of the building and peered over.

He could see and hear them plainly. Their voices were thick with anger—and fear.

Hawker listened to the many voices, all trying to talk at once.

". . . that's what I think we ought to do."

"Bullshit, man. I'll tell you who hit Fat Albert and Spooky. It was them Satanás, man. And if you ask me—"

"Cat Man said it was a *Casper*, motherfucker. Said it was a white boy that wasted the brothers. Shot his fucking dick off, man, so he should know."

"Yeah, and what about that weird drawing on the wall, man? Fucking big bird or somethin'. *Revenge* is what it said. This white dude be wanting revenge. Fucker's nuts, man. Cat Man say he didn't even *blink* before he hit 'em. Said he was cold as ice, man. Set it up so the cops think Cat Man did it—"

"Cat Man's crazy, blood. He's been doing his PCP thing too long. Don't be believin' that shit he talks. Razor the only man we listen to. The war council be meeting right now. So just hang loose. We got our leaders, man, and we follow our leaders. That the Panther way. Maybe you be a leader someday, little blood, then you know. Razor and Blade and Amin be deciding what we do. If they say we hit the Satanás, then we hit the Satanás. They say we go into Hillsboro and waste some Caspers, we do that, too. . . ."

On and on it went. Hawker tried to note all the

nicknames he heard. One of them he already recognized: "Razor." The other two, "Blade" and "Amin," were unfamiliar—but they sounded deadly.

Hawker looked forward to meeting all three.

The war party wasn't long in forming. Directly beneath Hawker cement steps led down into a basement stronghold.

Hawker guessed it was the Panthers' headquarters.

He heard a door swing open, then clank shut: a metal door.

Three men came out in single file. At first Hawker could only see the tops of their heads, then the backs of their heads. They wore jean jackets with the sleeves cut off, and blue bandannas tied around their necks. Hawker didn't have to guess at their nicknames. They were embroidered on the backs of their jackets.

Amin was well named. He had the black, fat gorilla face of the infamous dictator, Idi Amin. Hawker guessed him at six feet tall, close to three hundred pounds. He wore glistening black boots, and a chrome chain for a belt. His head was completely shaved. The glistening sweat on his face and head gave Amin the appearance of some massive creature who has just climbed out of a tar pit.

The gang leader named Blade was Amin's antithesis. Blade was small and wiry with a bushy black Afro, and the chilling grin of a man-child who is stunted emotionally and intellectually, frozen in the black-and-white world of childhood.

But there was nothing innocent about Blade's strange grin. It was the wolfish smile of a killer.

Of the three Razor was the most striking, the most impressive. He was tall and lithe, with something of a jungle cat in him. His movements were fluid and sure. His manner, perfunctory.

He was the man in charge. He knew it. They knew it. He had a strong, coffee-colored face and tiny piggish eyes. Hawker put him at six two, and maybe two hundred pounds of pure, corded muscle. His biceps rippled in the sleeveless jean jacket. The harsh vapor streetlights glinted off the rings on his fingers and the lone jeweled earring in his right ear.

When Razor, Amin, and Blade appeared, the other Panthers crowded around. Razor snapped his fingers and they were immediately silent.

"The lieutenants and me have worked this thing over in our heads," Razor began, surveying his troops. "I'm the one who talked to Cat Man in the hospital. I'm the one who heard his story. Dig? Cat Man says some Casper came to our turf and busted heads. Killed some of our own blood. Did worse to Cat Man."

The gang members muttered among themselves. Hawker listened intently, wondering where Razor was going.

"What I'm sayin', brothers, is that I'm not going to be doubting one of our own. Cat Man says it was this white dude—this Casper that drawed the big bird on the alley wall—then I ain't going to say he's lying. Dig? When the word comes from one of our own blood, then it's gospel. We don't lie to our own kind."

There were nods of approval from the others.

"But I will say this," Razor continued, now speaking louder. "Cat Man wasn't in too good a shape that night. He'd been doin' some shit—you all know what I'm saying. He'd been dusting his brains out, and I think the PCP finally done got to him. I think maybe one of them bad Satanás cats come to our turf and got down on our blood—that's what I think. This Sataná dude probably looked white, probably wasn't wearing his colors. . . ."

The Panthers were hooting their approval now.

"But just in case," Razor commanded above the other voices, "these are your orders: You find any Casper on our turf after dark, you kill him, dig? No talk, no questions—just *do* it. Cat Man says the dude had red hair. That's what you look for. Understand? If there really is some jive Casper cruising on our turf, we want to stop him and stop him quick. And I won't be happy until I got both his ears to add to my collection."

The Panthers laughed at that, nodding knowingly. There was something in their laughter which told Hawker that Razor really did have a collection of ears.

Razor continued: "But in the meantime—listen to me!—in the meantime I think we ought to jump into the war wagons and take a little cruise into Satanás turf!" Razor reached into his back pocket and produced a wicked-looking straight razor. He flicked open the blade and made a slashing motion. "Who's with me, blood? Who's got the balls to revenge our own?"

Amid yells and war cries the entire gang crammed into three broken-down station wagons and rattled off.

Amin drove the lead car, with Razor and Blade riding shotgun.

eight

When they were gone, Hawker found a fire-escape ladder at the back of the building. He climbed down and moved through the shadows to the street.

A few drunks were out, carrying their bottles in paper sacks. Traffic was light. Women sat on front steps, fanning themselves in the night heat.

Someone was bound to see him break into the Panthers' headquarters. And that was just what Hawker wanted—so long as they didn't try to stop him.

Hawker had no desire to injure the innocent. By the looks of things the residents of Starnsdale's black slums had already suffered enough.

The windows of the basement floor headquarters were barred and painted black—so no one could break in, or see in.

Hawker swung down the stairs. The door was

metal—as he'd suspected. They had snapped an industrial-weight padlock on it before they left.

From the small pack he carried Hawker took a thumb-sized chunk of plastic incendiary explosive. Hawker molded it around the lock and inserted the pyrotechnic blasting fuse.

Hawker lit the fuse and hugged the wall.

There was the *crack* of a rifle shot, and then the white-hot hissing of thermate. The lock glowed bright orange, then melted away.

Hawker, wearing a pair of thin leather driving gloves, swung the door open and flicked on the lights.

The Panthers' headquarters seemed to be a combination meetinghouse and warehouse.

Covering the floor were rows of television sets, tape recorders, kitchen appliances, bicycles, typewriters, and other odd goods. It took Hawker a moment to realize the stuff had all been stolen.

It was stored here, waiting to be fenced.

In the middle of the room was a long folding-table. There were empty beer bottles on the table, and the ashtrays were stuffed full. The walls were covered with psychedelic posters proclaiming soul singers, or demanding black power.

Hawker took two blue bugs from his pouch and tore off the adhesive strips on each. He hid one behind a Jimmy Hendrix poster and the other beside a wad of gum beneath the table.

In the far corner of the room was a metal desk with drawers. Kneeling beside it, Hawker found the drawers locked. He wondered how big a business gang-theft was. Big enough to keep files?

Hawker got down on the floor and rolled on his back so he could see the bottom of the desk. First he stuck another little blue bug on the base of the desk. Then he went to work on the steel rod that held the drawers locked. It took him a few minutes to slide it out.

The files were surprisingly neat. But they weren't labeled. Hawker began to riffle through the papers. A sheet of names caught his attention.

It was a membership list, complete with ages, addresses, and a few phone numbers.

A street gang with a membership list?

Razor was beginning to impress him. He was not only a leader but an organizer as well.

It was a dangerous combination.

A deep voice startled him. It came from the doorway.

"Somebody in here, I'll guarantee you that, man."

Another voice agreed. "Shit—looka here. Burned the fucking lock right off."

"Razor ain't gonna like this shit. He told us to keep an eye on things. We best do somethin'."

"Yeah. An' I'll tell you just what we do, man. We go in there and kill any motherfucker we see."

Hawker pulled the big Colt Commander .45 out of its holster and hid behind the desk as the door swung open.

Hawker didn't like what he saw. The two men were older than the others. Early thirties. But each wore a blue bandanna around his neck.

The lead man carried a sawed-off 12-gauge. A pump gun. The other held a feminine-looking automatic in his right hand.

They moved slowly into the room, their eyes searching.

"These lights ain't supposed to be on, man. There's somebody in here just as sure as shit."

"Shut up, man! Just keep your eyes open, fool."

"Maybe we ought to call the cops."

"*Cops?* Are you nuts, man? Cops get in here and see all this shit, and all our asses will be in prison. Now just shut that stupid head of yours and look, man."

Hawker crouched lower as they came toward him. On the floor near the desk was a beer bottle. Hawker waited until they were both looking away. He tossed the bottle toward the far side of the room. When they whirled at the sound of the crash, Hawker stood.

"Freeze, assholes! I'll blow your heads off if you so much as blink. Now, toss those weapons away."

The two men stood like statues. They hesitated before dropping their guns. Hawker drew back the hammer of the Colt. The sound of the hammer was like a command. They tossed their weapons away.

"Now turn toward me—slowly," demanded Hawker.

The man who had held the automatic was visibly nervous. His eyes darted from Hawker to the open door. Hawker wondered if he might be thinking of bolting toward freedom. He moved between the two men and the door.

The man who had carried the shotgun had dark, fierce eyes and an ugly expression. He was the spokesman, and Hawker let him talk.

"You're the dude who wasted Fat Albert and Spooky, and shot Cat Man," he said. It wasn't a question. It was a statement. The man's voice revealed no fear. Only contempt.

"That's right," said Hawker.

A light sneer crossed the man's face. "You're dead, white boy. Right now you're breathin' and your heart's beating, but you're a goner. The walking dead, that's what you are. The Panthers are going to be hunting you, white boy. And you can't run far enough."

"Pretty brave talk for a man with a .45 pointed at his head."

The sneer broadened. "Things change, white boy. Things about to change right now, matter of fact." He looked toward the open door. "Ain't that right, Charlie?"

Hawker sensed it was a trick. He didn't look toward the door. He should have.

"I got me a little ol' .38 pointed right at your back, mister-man," said an unfamiliar voice. "You best be tossing that pretty silver gun of yours on the floor."

Hawker glanced over his shoulder. A hugely fat black man filled the doorway. He dwarfed the revolver in his right hand.

Hawker let the Colt Commander fall by his feet.

"Kick that pretty gun away, mister-man. Kick it away or I'll drop you where you stand."

Hawker shoved the gun with his foot. The man with the ugly sneer picked it up, inspected it, then slapped Hawker with the back of his hand so unexpectedly that Hawker didn't have time to react.

"Like I told you, white boy." He chuckled. "You're heart's beatin', but you're dead." He looked at the others. "Might as well have some fun before he die, eh, fellas?"

Without waiting for a reply, the man drew a cheap case knife from his pocket and locked it open. "Razor be wantin' your ears for his collection," he said as he walked toward Hawker. "And I reckon Cat Man would be real pleased if we sent him your balls in a box. Nice little white balls, eh?"

The other two laughed heartily.

Hawker waited as the man approached, the knife held loose and ready. The man who had surprised him, Charlie, had closed the door. He was about two arm lengths behind him. The third man had retrieved the shotgun and now held it on Hawker.

Hawker had one thing going for him: Both men were directly in each other's line of fire. Anyone that stupid, he knew, could be beaten.

The man with the knife lunged at him. Instead of jumping back, Hawker knocked the knife aside and locked his left arm over the man's right elbow.

With his fist flattened into a cutting edge Hawker smashed the man's windpipe closed and swung him into Charlie as, at the same moment, he dived toward the shotgun.

There was the roar of a gunshot by his ear, followed by a scream. Hawker didn't have time to see what had happened. He wrestled the shotgun away, dived, rolled, and came up in time to see that the man who had lost the shotgun now held his own Colt Commander.

Hawker didn't hesitate. He fired, pumped, and fired again.

The first shot drove the man across the room. The second shot blew his face away.

After pumping a fresh round into the chamber, Hawker surveyed the room.

Charlie lay dead in his own blood. He had been hit by the first shotgun blast intended for Hawker.

The man with the knife still kicked pathetically on the floor, his eyes bulging. Hawker watched as the man clawed frantically at his ruined throat, then went slack and empty. Dead.

Hawker didn't like what he was about to do. But it was something the Panthers would understand.

More important, it was something that would both frighten them and earn their respect.

He took the knife from the hand of the dead man—the man who had tried to cut Hawker.

Kneeling beside the corpse, Hawker sliced and sawed through the tough cartilage of the man's left ear. It finally pulled away with a rooty tearing sound.

Hawker carried the ear to the smooth surface of the desk. Using the blood like paint, he drew the head of a hawk.

And in rough block letters he wrote: FOR YOUR COLLECTION.

He left the ear on the desk and switched out the lights.

nine

Hawker knew he had to hurry.

The Panthers had gone to declare war on the Satanás. And the Satanás didn't strike Hawker as the type to back down from anything.

So there would be a fight. A big fight—probably on neutral ground.

Hawker wanted to make it to the Satanás' headquarters, break in, bug it, then get out before they returned.

It was ten forty-three P.M. by the green glow of his Seiko.

He drove quickly through the Sunday streets of Hillsboro, headed for the Latin section. He had left his bloodied leather gloves hidden in an alley garbage can. The steering wheel was slick in his hands.

He slowed and swung east on Ybor Avenue.

The customized low-rider cars cavorted in the slow lane. Hawker passed them without looking back.

Teen-agers roamed the streets, carrying their ghetto blasters—huge portable radios. They snapped their fingers as they half-walked, half-danced down their personal corridors of hell.

Hawker wondered what became of such teen-agers—knowing what became of them even as he wondered.

Raised too often by unwed mothers who really didn't give a damn about them, they did poorly in school and they fared even worse in the world's work force. They grew up as vicious as the vicious slum society that produced them.

Their lives would become a series of easy choices on the road to social slavery: welfare, drugs, crime, and, most probably, the outlaw fellowship of a street gang.

So far Hawker had done battle only with adult members of the Panthers and Satanás. They were full-grown men; men old enough to know right from wrong. With them it was kill or be killed.

As he drove, Hawker wondered about the kids in the gangs—for he had seen kids in both groups, teen-age boys hardly old enough to shave.

If they came at him with murder in their eyes, would he be able to squeeze the trigger?

Hawker wondered. He also wondered if there wasn't some way he could prevent it.

He drove past the Satanás' headquarters twice. Lights were on inside, but no one was there. The outline of a hawk's head, he noticed, was still seared into the wall.

They wouldn't soon forget.

Hawker decided he had to make use of what little time he had. Instead of parking on the Hillsboro edge of the slums, Hawker pulled into a side street and got out.

He pulled the black watch-cap low over his head and patted the Colt Commander to make sure it was safely holstered beneath his shirt. He slung the canvas pack over his shoulder and moved off through the shadows.

It was eleven ten P.M.

Hawker wondered how long the two gangs would battle.

The door of the Satanás' headquarters swung open easily. It surprised him—and made him even more cautious.

The main room was brightly lighted. The walls were covered with bold, bright *placas*—street graffiti, in elaborate script. There were seedy lounge chairs against the walls, a main table, a television, and a telephone.

It looked as if they had left in a hurry. An ashtray still smoldered. Half-full bottles of beer rested on the table and on the cement floor.

Hawker could picture the Panthers idling by in their "war wagons," calling out a challenge, and then the Satanás racing off in pursuit.

If that was the scenario, they had probably been at it for nearly half an hour.

Hawker would have to hurry. If the whole gang

came back at once, he would be trapped. And to be trapped by the Satanás meant death.

Quickly he unscrewed the mouthpiece of the telephone and connected a yellow disc-shaped three-wire listening device. He wiped his prints from the phone and placed it as he had found it.

From the canvas pack he took three more blue bugs and stripped off the adhesive covers. He stuck one under the desk, another under the middle lounge chair, and the third in the grimy, closet-size toilet.

There was a wooden door at the back of the main room. It was padlocked on a rusted hinge. Hawker drew the Commander, then kicked open the door.

The room was dark and musty. Hawker felt along the wall and finally found the light switch.

It was a storeroom. Like the Panthers, the Satanás had their own warehouse of stolen goods. Televisions and stereos were packed almost to the ceiling. There was enough stuff for Hawker to know that the street gang ranged a lot farther than Hillsboro to do their stealing. It looked as though they had been hitting every suburb in L.A.

Hawker made his way through the rows of merchandise. In the far corner of the room was an old steel file cabinet. Hawker jerked the drawers open, one by one.

Nothing.

That's when he noticed the safe: an old khaki floor safe, as squat and heavy as a miniature bulldozer.

Hawker took a half-handful of the claylike thermate composition. He squeezed it into the seams of the safe, then added the pyrotechnic fuse. He ignited it and turned away.

The thermate burned with white-hot intensity— 2,150 degrees Centigrade—for almost a minute.

The armor-plated door jolted beneath its own unsupported weight, then crashed to the floor.

Hawker knelt by the safe and looked inside. The bottom was covered with a small stack of folders. Hawker jammed them into his sack and then began going through the wooden drawers of the safe.

He expected to find money. He didn't. Instead, he found five one-pound-sized bags of white powder. He sniffed it but didn't taste it. Only amateurs and TV cops are stupid enough to taste an unidentified substance.

Hawker guessed it to be heroin.

He finished going through the rest of the drawers, then carried the bags of white powder to the toilet. He dumped them in and flushed twice.

He was about to shut off the light when he heard footsteps.

"Hey—who's in there? That you, Hammer? Hey— Jesús?" It was a squawky, adolescent voice thick with a Spanish accent.

Hawker listened as the footsteps came closer. He hugged the wall, waiting.

When he saw the shadow cover the doorway, he reached out and rammed the intruder against the wall, the Colt Commander jammed against his left ear.

"Shit, mister, don't kill me; please don't kill me."

Hawker realized that the voice came from a slightly built teen-ager. The kid was tall but thin—probably sixteen years old at the most. He had a bright, olive-colored face, and he wore the red bandanna of the Satanás.

The kid seemed to focus on him for the first time. His eyes widened, as if he were seeing his first big league ballplayer. "Hey, you're *him*. You're the gringo . . . the red-haired one who—" His eyes changed from wonder to terror. "You're the gringo who pisses fire!"

Hawker released his grip. "I should kill you," he whispered.

"No, no—please don't kill me."

"Then talk. And talk fast."

"Anything, mister. I'll tell you anything."

"Tell me about your gang. Tell me about your leaders. Who are they, what are they like? Where do you fence the stuff you steal? And how many more kids your age are in the gang?"

Hawker didn't have to prod him again. The kid told him all he wanted to know and more, in a rapid, rattling English.

When he had finished, Hawker backed a step away. The kid seemed to sag with relief. Hawker couldn't help feeling a little sorry for him.

"What's your name?"

"My nickname is Caña—it means 'cane,' 'cause

I'm so thin. My real name is Julio Castanada
Balserio."

"You seem like a nice kid, Julio, so tell me: Why
in the hell did you join the Satanás?"

He shrugged. "You fight them. Or you join
them." He shrugged again. "I am not stupid."

Hawker nodded. "I'm not going to kill you,
Julio. But tell your friends that I am looking for
them. And tell your leaders that I'll kill them if
they don't kill me first."

Hawker went to the front door and glanced
both ways. The road was clear. Hawker went out
the door.

"Hey—gringo," the voice of Julio Castanada
Balserio called after him. "They say you are the
devil. Is it true?"

Hawker turned down the street at an easy trot.
His voice echoed behind him.

"It's true. . . ."

ten

_____

When Hawker got back to his cottage on Manhattan Beach, he hid his weaponry, then steamed himself clean in the shower.

It was twelve thirty-five A.M.

He set the teakettle on to boil. A chilly summer wind blew off the Pacific, rustling the curtains. The sound of the sea breaking over the reef was like a waterfall.

Hawker dressed himself in fresh socks and a favorite pair of sweat pants. It was cool enough for a sweater, and Hawker pulled a worn cotton crewneck over his head.

When the kettle whistled, he steeped a bag of Emperor's Choice herb tea in a stoneware mug. He added honey, then carried the mug to the porch, where he had placed the Eavesdrop receiver.

Hawker keyed the rewind toggle, then hit the

forward switch. The circuit-one tape had recorded every sound in the Panthers' headquarters, beginning with his starting the car as he drove to the slums, and then the muffled explosion of Hawker's breaking in.

Hawker let the tape play completely through. He heard the gunshots and the hoarse death cries of the men he had killed. There was a momentary silence on the tape, and then the noise of the other Panthers returning as the machine began to record again.

He listened to that segment carefully, making notes in his mind.

The Eavesdrop had begun recording in midconversation—presumably, as the street gang leaders came through the door.

". . . done broke into our fucking headquarters—"

"We been hit, man!"

"Some brothers dead in here, Razor! Fuckin' corpses everywhere, man!"

There was the static garble then of many voices calling at once. Then the cold, calm voice of Razor, their leader, took control.

"Shut up! You hear me? Now, shut that damn door. You want someone to see in here, fool? Amin, you go outside and tell the other bloods go on home. Don't say nothin' 'bout this shit."

"Razor—look at this, man. They done cut off his fucking ear!"

"Son of a—"

"Here it is. Aw, shit. It's that Hawk business—"

"The fucking ear is on the *desk*, man. Got a

message in fucking *blood*. Says you're supposed to
add this ear to your collection, Razor. Written in
blood—"

"Get out of my way, fool!"

"Who the fuck is this Hawk dude, Razor?
Couldn't be with the Satanás. Hell, we was
heads-up with the Satanás when this dude was in
here—"

"Maybe Cat Man's right, Razor. Maybe it's this
white dude with the red hair. He's a fucking
killer, man—"

"I'm startin' to get a little nervous, Razor, no
shit, man. This dude is bad news. Like a lunatic
or somethin'—"

". . . his throat's been crushed, man. Look the
way his eyes be bugging out—"

"Quiet! Y'all just shut up, hear? Man can't hear
himself think. How'd this dude know where to hit
us? That's what I want to know. Anybody got an
answer to that? And how'd this dude know we was
gonna be out? And how in the fuck did he know
about my ear collection, unless—"

"Shit, Razor, you don't think one of our bloods
has gone over to whitey, do you? Like an informer—"

"Somebody been talking, damn it! That's the
one thing that's clear here, man. This white dude
been getting information from somebody. And I'll
tell you this: If I find out who it is, they're dead.
I'll kill them myself, and they ain't gonna die
easy—"

"This shit's starting to get spooky, Razor. Maybe we ought to cool it for a few weeks. Close down—"

"Close down, my ass! We gonna find this informer, and we gonna kill him. Then we gonna find this Hawk dude, and we gonna kill him, too."

"How in the hell—"

"No more talk, man! We got work to do. We got to get these TVs and shit out of here. Got to hide everything someplace else. And then we got to call the cops."

"Gonna call the cops?"

"And what the fuck would *you* do, man? Try and hide three bodies in downtown L.A.? You nuts? They'll pin all this shit on us, if we do. Gotta get the cops in. Cat Man told 'em the story about this Hawk dude, and they didn't believe him. Maybe they'll believe him now. . . ."

Hawker switched off the machine and sipped his tea. He had heard at least six different voices on the tape. To him it meant that, no matter what Razor commanded, the word would, indeed, get out to the rest of the Panthers.

Their reaction, he hoped, would be even more emotional than that of their leaders.

All the elements Hawker wanted were there: fear, panic, and loss of confidence.

The Panthers were heading for a fall. A very hard fall. Now Hawker was concerned about the few—the very few—who didn't deserve to fall.

Hawker remembered what the young Satanà, Julio Balserio, had told him: "You fight them. Or you join them."

Hawker wanted to give kids like Balserio a chance to get out. It wouldn't be easy to arrange. But it was important that he try.

Hawker backed the second tape and switched the Eavesdrop unit to circuit two. He used fast forward to skip the noise he had made, then listened as the Satanás returned.

The exclamations of surprise were in a profane mixture of English and Spanish—shock similar to that which he had heard in the Panthers' headquarters.

Then the recorder picked up the adolescent voice of Julio Balserio—Caña, to the other Satanás. Julio spoke in English.

". . . saw him, cuz. He put a gun to my head. Said he'd kill me—"

"Who the hell was it, Caña? And you'd better have a damn good reason for letting this *cabrón*—"

"The gringo; the gringo who hit us the other night, Hammer! He's the one that broke in here and tore the place apart. He's the devil, Hammer. I swear to God he's evil—"

There was the sound of someone being slapped, and then Julio began to cry.

"Don't hit me no more, Hammer. I couldn't do nothing. He'd already torn the place up by the time I found him."

"Shit! Hammer, he blew open the fucking safe! He took the junk, man!"

The voices on the tape became muffled then. Hawker realized how stupid he'd been not to bug the storeroom. He could understand brief snatches of distant yelling, but nothing more. Soon, though, they returned to the meeting room. Julio was no longer crying, but the fear was still evident in his voice. He was reenacting what had happened.

". . . door was open, so I came in. I kept calling for you, Hammer. And for Jesús. I didn't know you was out gang-banging with the Panthers. Got here by the toilet, and he just *appeared*. Like out of nowhere, he was just *there*. Like a ghost or something."

"You fuckin' nuts, Caña. Ain't no such things as—"

"Let our little cuz talk, man! I seen that son of a bitch piss fire. You saw it, too. We got some scary shit on our hands here, Hammer."

"Just a trick, man. That was just some sort of gringo trick—"

"Keep talking, Caña. What happened next?"

"He grabbed me by the shirt and slammed me into the wall. I tried to fight him, Hammer. Smacked him good a couple of times. But it was like my fists went right through him. And you know how hard I can hit!"

There was laughter and a few profane observations.

"Shut up! So what happened after you hit the gringo, Caña?"

"He just sorta laughed at me. Like he knew I couldn't hurt him. Then he pulls out this big silver pistol—like no gun I've ever seen. I mean, it was like it was on *fire*! Put it to my head, and it was hot, man. Real hot."

"What did he say, Caña? And you best tell us the truth—"

"I ain't lying to you, Hammer! I wouldn't lie to a cuz."

"Then you better not. What happened next?"

Caña hesitated, formulating his lie. "He . . . he gave me a message to give to you, Hammer. Called you by name! He knows all about us, Hammer—everything, man. Mentioned Jesús and Matador and Lobo, too! Like magic—"

"What was the message, Caña?"

"He said: 'Tell Hammer and the rest that I'm going to destroy them. Tell them I'm going to take them back to hell.'" There was the sound of a scuffle, and Julio began to cry again. "Don't be hittin' me no more, Hammer! I'm tellin' the truth, damn it. Don't be blaming me for what the Hawk did. He's wicked, man. I tried to fight him, Hammer, but he's too wicked, man. He told me himself—he's the *devil*!"

Hawker switched off the set and finished his tea. He carried the Eavesdrop unit back into the cottage. He set the recorder and armed the receiver.

It was ready to record conversations in both street-gang headquarters.

Suddenly Hawker felt very tired. It was just after one A.M. He considered finishing his work in the morning, but he decided there wasn't time. He would have to work far into the night because there were too many unknowns. Too many factors he had yet to uncover.

Of one thing he was sure: There was more to these two street gangs than just violence-hungry kids.

Their operations were too well-organized. Their scores too big. It takes money to buy five bags of heroin. Big, big money—and complicated connections, as well.

The Satanás were into more than just street crime. Maybe the Panthers, too.

Hawker switched on the fluorescent light over his desk. He took out a pen and a blank notebook. As he read through the files he had stolen from the Panthers and the Satanás, he began to make notes. Occasionally he gave a light whistle of surprise.

When he was done with the files, he booted his computer and dialed the State Crime Information Center in L.A. He requested information on a list of ten names.

After a few seconds of scanning, the SCIC banks marched data in lime-green letters across Hawker's computer screen.

Only one name surprised him.

When he was done, Hawker switched off his computer and turned again to his notebook. He wanted the hierarchy of the street gangs clear in his own mind.

Using only their nicknames, Hawker made a list:

PANTHERS

Razor: Chieftain. Twenty-seven. Arrests numerous. Suspect in three murders. One conviction: rape. Three months served in a detention

center. Takes nickname from favorite weapon:
straight razor. Known drug user.

Amin: Lieutenant. Twenty-four. Arrests numerous. Considers himself a political revolu-
tionary. At age twelve turned over to authorities
for torturing schoolmate. Released after therapy.
Convicted of armed robbery and assault, 1981.
Paroled. Known drug addict.

Blade: Lieutenant. Twenty-two. Arrests numerous. Suspect in one murder, three rapes.
No convictions. As nickname suggests, uses a
knife. Considered extremely dangerous by Los
Angeles police. Known drug user.

SATANÁS

Hammer: Chieftain. Age unknown. Puerto
Rican mother, anglo father. Arrests numerous.
Suspect in the sledgehammer murder of L.A.
businessman. Case dismissed. No convictions.

Matador: Lieutenant. Twenty-six. Known for
flashy dress and good looks. Considers himself
an actor. Arrests numerous. Identified by eyewitness as suspect in a 1981 rape/murder case.
Case dismissed due to prosecutor's error. No
convictions. Known drug user.

Jesús: Lieutenant. Twenty-four. One arrest,
Considers himself a political activist and a
racial/religious prophet. Suspect in the double
mutilation murder of two L.A. prostitutes. Released after questioning.

Lobo: Lieutenant. Nineteen. Three arrests.
Arm withered by polio as child. Known sexual
deviant. Convicted of sodomy and child molest-
ing at age fifteen. Six months in detention center;
twelve months of therapy. Released. Considered extremely dangerous by Los Angeles police.

Hawker finished the list, then tossed the pen down, disgusted. Somewhere he had read that nations live under the governments they deserve. Hawker wondered how voters and politicians could have allowed the courts to degenerate to the point where such animals were allowed to freely roam the streets.

It was not a new topic of thought. He had been shocked and disgusted by the leniency of the liberal justice system during his years as a Chicago cop. It was a primary reason why he'd resigned.

Once again he wondered if it was because the judges and politicians were naive—or if it was because they really believed the rights of the criminal are more important than the rights of potential victims.

Whatever the reason it sickened Hawker. And he couldn't help believing that a large percentage of Americans felt exactly as he did.

His only comfort was in knowing that the animals listed in his notebook would not go free.

For once they would be made to suffer for the suffering they had caused.

For once they would be given swift and just punishment.

Though they didn't know it, they had already been sentenced to death. . . .

eleven

She came to him in the night, smelling of body
powder and shampoo.

Hawker heard the screen door swing shut as he
lay in his bed. He padded naked to the living
room. Melanie St. John stood in the darkness.
Her breasts were erect mounds beneath the filmy
material of her nightgown.

"I missed you," she whispered. "I'm sorry . . .
if I woke you."

She slipped comfortably into Hawker's arms,
warm against his skin.

"I tried to call you. You were out."

"I had a busy night," said Hawker, yawning.

"Out looking for work, right?"

"Right."

She tangled his hair in her right hand and pulled
his lips hard against hers. Her tongue was hot and

alive against his. Her soft fingers traced the geometric chunks of muscle on Hawker's stomach, then slid downward, finding Hawker with her small hand.

"My, you are aggressive tonight, woman."

She smiled vampishly. "You don't seem like the kind of man who's intimidated by aggressive women."

"What do you think?"

She squeezed him. "Umm . . . you don't feel intimidated." She kissed him again, harder, then whispered in his ear. "I'm tired of being treated like something special, Hawk. That's why I like you. To you I'm just another woman."

"Maybe you are something special, Melanie."

"Not tonight, I'm not. Tonight I'm . . . feeling wicked."

"Is *that* what they call that thing you're feeling?"

She trembled as she laughed. "I'm sick of being treated like a great lady, Hawk."

"Oh?"

"Yes. I want you . . . I want you to fuck me . . . fuck me any way you want; make it as rough as you want. Treat me like the lowest whore in creation, because I feel like a whore tonight. I want you to fuck me tonight, Hawk . . . please, now . . . and hard . . . if you're man enough."

Trying not to look as amused as he felt, Hawker lifted her into his arms. She had demanded he play a role. An interesting role—but a theatrical part nonetheless. It was sexual playtime, and Hawker had been given the caveman costume.

Deciding it was better than a bit part on *CHiPs*,
Hawker carried her to the bedroom and threw her
roughly on the bed.

Hawker loomed over her for a moment, mus-
cles glistening. Her back arched, and her soft
mound of pubic hair lifted as he ripped her gown
away and shot it against the wall.

Throwing things was part of the role.

"Yes," she whispered. "That's what I want. Take
me, Hawk, fuck me. Use me any way you want."

As Hawker shoved her over onto her stomach
and slapped her thighs wide, her buttocks lifted,
moist and open.

"Oh, yes," she moaned. "From behind . . . *yes*
. . . deep inside me, Hawk . . ."

Hawker climbed onto the bed, kneeling behind
her. He glanced idly at his watch.

It was three fifteen.

Hawker wondered if people in California ever
took time to sleep. . . .

Only half-awake, Hawker felt the woman kiss
him gently on the cheek and get out of bed.

"That was wonderful, darling," she whispered.
"I'm going to get a glass of water. Want some?"

"Yeah," grumbled Hawker. "In the morning.
With my breakfast."

She laughed and patted him. Hawker heard her
walk cautiously across the room, then fumble for
the light switch.

The glare of light and the scream were simul-
taneous. Hawker jolted upright. It took him a long

minisecond to focus, and then understand what he saw.

A man stood in the bedroom doorway. He had a greasy red beard and long, peroxide-bleached hair.

Melanie had crumpled back against the wall, her hands at her mouth, terrified.

The man had something in his hand. It was a gun. Slowly, almost as if he were enjoying it, he leveled the revolver at Hawker.

There was a tight smile on his lips.

"Present from a friend," said the man with the red beard.

Hawker's hand swept under the pillow. Shots thudded into the bed behind him as he rolled onto the floor.

Hawker hugged the floor, waiting—the little Walther automatic cold in his hand.

As the man came around the bed, Hawker took the first target presented. He squeezed the trigger twice, and the man's kneecap exploded.

The man collapsed backward. His scream was more like a hiss.

Hawker stood, the Walther fused between his two big hands. Red Beard had one hand wrapped around his knee in agony.

In the other hand he still held the revolver. His eyes seemed to focus through the pain, and another shot smashed into the wall over Hawker's head.

Hawker didn't hesitate. He squeezed off one careful round. An ember-red eye suddenly appeared on Red Beard's forehead. The eye began to spout blood. Red Beard's hands quivered. The revolver fell heavily on the carpet.

Melanie St. John began to scream. The scream was like the wail of a siren.

Hawker went to her and shook her gently. "It's okay," he said calmly. "It's over. He's dead."

The woman shook herself, breathing heavily. "You . . . you *killed* him."

"It seemed like the thing to do."

"He's *dead*."

"Unless he's a hell of an actor, yes."

Hawker helped the woman to her feet. He went to the kitchen, flipping on lights as he went. He brought her the water she had wanted, then sat her down on the bed beside the phone.

"Can you talk? Coherently, I mean."

She couldn't take her eyes off the corpse. Hawker shook her again, "Hey, listen to me. I want you to call the police. Have the operator connect you."

She buried her face in her hands and began to weep softly. Hawker stroked her hair. "Never mind," he said. "I'll do it myself. But first I want to go out and have a look around. Our friend might have a partner."

Hawker pulled on his running shorts and a pair of leather sandals. Carrying the Walther, he made two slow trips around the cottage.

The dark, indifferent sea still roared over the reef. A dog barked in the distance, and there was the sound of faraway traffic. Hawker found nothing.

He went back inside. Melanie sat on the porch. She had found Hawker's robe, and she held the collar tight around her neck. A bottle of Scotch sat on the table beside her. The tumbler she held was half full.

"No one out there. He was alone, I guess."

"My God, it's like a bad dream." She gave him a pathetic look of helplessness. "It's not a dream, is it, James?"

"No. I wish it were. But it's not. Did you know the guy?"

"No. I didn't know him."

There was a moment's hesitation before she answered. Hawker didn't press it. He went into the kitchen, opened a bottle of beer, then picked up the phone.

The information operator offered him the LAPD emergency number. Hawker asked for the dispatch desk instead.

A man answered. Hawker asked to be connected with homicide. As the phone rang, Hawker heard the electronic beep which informed him the conversation was being recorded.

"Homicide. Lieutenant Detective Flaherty."

"My name is Hawker, Lieutenant. A man broke into my rental cottage fifteen minutes ago. He shot at me, and I returned fire. He's dead."

Hawker gave his telephone number and his address. He hung up and went out to the porch.

Melanie studied him for a moment. She held up the tumbler. It was almost empty. "My first drink in almost two months."

"Tonight I think you can consider it medicine. A sedative. Maybe you ought to have another."

She shook her head and turned the tumbler upside down on the table. "Not now. Not tomorrow. Not ever."

"You have a will of iron, woman."

She gave a derisive chuckle. "I acted like your typical hysterical twelve-year-old in there, James. You know it. I know it. And I'm ashamed. If it had been a movie, I'd have been in complete control. You would have turned to me, whimpering for support. After all the times I've played that role, I'd actually sort of come to believe it." The bitter laugh slipped from her lips again. "Now I know just what a silly fool I am."

"So you're human. Wait here while I call the *National Enquirer*. The world will be shocked and disappointed. For Christ's sake, Melanie, give yourself a break. Thankfully, very few people ever see another human being die violently. When it happens, most well-adjusted people go right into shock. It's nothing to be ashamed of."

Her eyes locked onto Hawker's. "You didn't. You didn't go into shock." When he didn't react to the implied question, she continued, "But, then, most people don't keep guns under their pillows, either. You do, though. And you know how to use it, too. I watched you, James. I saw everything like it was in horrible slow motion. You knew exactly what you were doing when you shot him. Your eyes didn't even blink." She stood and touched his face, looking deep into him. "Why won't you trust me, James? Are you still a cop? Hell, I don't care if you're a cop. I love you anyway. Are you in trouble? Maybe I can help."

Hawker took her arms and swung her gently back into the chair. "I'm neither, Melanie. It's a long story, and maybe I'll tell you about it when we're both bored and have nothing else to do. But right now, from the sound of those sirens, I'd say the cops are about four blocks away. I want you to go home. Now. If you stay, they're going to ask you a lot of embarrassing questions, and the press is going to get wind of it, and you'll be in for a hell of a lot of bad publicity."

"No," she said firmly. "I'm staying."

"Damn it, Melanie, I know about this stuff."

"Damn it yourself, Hawk! I know a little bit about how things work myself. I'm no empty-headed blonde. I was an eyewitness, and having an eyewitness is going to save you a lot of time and trouble."

Hawker smiled. "You're sure?"

Her voice was right out of a 1940s detective movie. "Just sit down and shut up, ya big lug. Leave everything to me. I'll twist those screws around my little finger."

twelve

Lieutenant Detective Walter Flaherty, as Hawker soon learned, wasn't the kind of man easily twisted around anyone's finger.

He pulled up in an unmarked Ford behind the two squad cars, all three skidding to a halt on the sandy side street.

Flaherty was the last to get out. He wore a summer-weight tweed jacket and wrinkled slacks. He had the plain, benign face of a country priest. Thin brown, curly hair was visible beneath the woven Sussex hat that was pulled low—as if he expected rain. Flaherty had the overall appearance of a peaceful man on a European fishing vacation. He looked like a dull little clerk who wanted nothing more than to sit in some anonymous house and watch his children grow.

Except for his eyes. Hawker took one look at

the man's eyes and knew he would have to tread carefully. They were gray-green prisms that reflected shrewdness and wit and bulldog tenacity. Hawker felt the eyes survey him as the uniformed cops brushed by them to check the corpse. Flaherty nodded, studied Melanie St. John until he seemed satisfied that he recognized her, then followed the cops into the bedroom.

Hawker stayed on the porch with the woman. She seemed nervous. Hawker caught her eye. "Just tell the truth," he said.

"And what else would I tell them?"

"I have a feeling you've seen the guy who broke in here before, Melanie. No, don't argue, now. If I'm wrong, I'm wrong. But if you did lie to me—for whatever reason—don't lie to Flaherty. I've seen his kind before. He'll give you all kinds of rope—then come back a few days later and use it to choke you. Think about it."

Flaherty had returned to the porch so quietly that he surprised even Hawker. He had both hands stuffed into his pants pockets, and he rocked calmly back and forth on the balls of his feet as he talked.

"Yes, the man is indeed quite dead. Nasty case of bullet in the head," he said. "You're James Hawker? The gentleman who called?"

"That's right."

"This is your house?"

"I'm leasing it."

"Have you been here long?"

"Less than a week. I'm from Chicago. I'm thinking of moving to California."

"The man broke in and you shot him?"

"I did. He opened fire on me first. I was very lucky. I still can't quite believe it really happened."

Flaherty rocked forward on his toes, and pursed his lips as if about to whistle. "Yes," he said. "A great shock to the average peace-loving vacationer, I suppose." He looked at Hawker and smiled. "And to you, too, Miss Melanie St. John. Yes, I recognize you. And who wouldn't? I must admit to being a great fan of yours. Yes, it's true. In fact my dear wife, Irene, becomes quite jealous when I go to one of your movies—can you imagine? And me the father of four lovely daughters. Not a son to my name, but I couldn't be happier. I sometimes chide my daughters by referring to them as 'my four misses.' "

Immediately put at ease by Flaherty, Melanie's laughter was genuine. Hawker wanted to warn her once again to be careful. He didn't get the chance. "Mr. Hawker, would you mind if I questioned Miss St. John alone? I'd ask her to sit in the car with me, but the impropriety of that—what with Irene being already a bit jealous . . ."

Hawker stood. "I can go for a walk outside."

Flaherty disapproved—but diplomatically. "It might be better if you waited in the cottage. Wouldn't want an accomplice to get you—ha ha. Oh, and close the door behind you, Mr. Hawker."

Hawker found a book and read as the cops worked in the bedroom. They traced the outline of the corpse on the floor in blue chalk. They measured the distance between the dead man and the bullet holes in the bed and wall. The lab truck arrived, and they lifted a selection of fingerprints. Hawker's Walther and the dead man's revolver were dutifully placed in plastic sacks and labeled. They gave Hawker a receipt.

A coroner's wagon pulled up and they carted the body away. Hawker followed the gurney onto the porch and was surprised to find that Flaherty was alone, going over his notes.

"Ah, Mr. Hawker." He smiled. "I was just about to call you. Miss St. John was very tired, so I suggested she go home and go to bed."

"Very thoughtful of you, Lieutenant," Hawker said wryly.

"Uh, oh. Something in your voice, Mr. Hawker, tells me I may have stood in the way of romance."

"Not at all—"

One of the policemen interrupted, asking for instructions. Flaherty dismissed him with perfunctory orders about reports in the afternoon.

Hawker recognized it as a premeditated move to leave the two of them alone.

"Drink, Lieutenant?"

"Drink as in 'alcohol'?"

"I've got some herb tea."

"Ah, that would be very nice. One week out of every four I have to work the late shift, and I've always had trouble sleeping during the day. My wife says it's because of the coffee I drink. Irene would approve of herb tea. With honey, if you have it."

Hawker put water on. He changed into a shirt

and pants while it heated. He steeped the tea in mugs, and carried the mugs onto the porch.

Flaherty took it appreciatively. "So tell me, Mr. Hawker, how long were you a policeman? Or perhaps you still are?"

Hawker sat opposite him, trying not to look surprised. "Did Melanie tell you to ask that?"

"Not at all, not at all." Flaherty sipped at his tea. "I get so bored when I work the late shift that I make myself play little games of deduction—to keep my mind alert, you see. I wasn't blessed with the quick wit some of my fellow officers have, so I must work at it."

"I'll bet," Hawker said dryly.

"No, it's true. But, all modesty aside, I really am getting quite good at it. I'll let you be the judge." Flaherty straightened himself in the chair, as if about to recite in school. "Let's see if I can get it all straight. Yes. A stranger breaks into your house. He tries to kill you, but you kill him instead. Like a good citizen, you immediately notify the police. But do you call the emergency number? No."

"Why tie up the emergency line?" Hawker asked in defense. "Someone really in trouble could have been trying to call. The man was dead. It was no longer an emergency."

Flaherty held up one finger in exclamation. "Exactly. You called the main desk and asked to be transferred to homicide. Your statement to me was a model of clarity. Just the right amount of information in just the right order. No gasping and crying, no confused rhetoric about the horror of killing, and no feverish plea to believe that you had absolutely no choice—all of which one might expect from the common citizen." Flaherty put his tea down and smiled. "Don't you see the many opportunities for deduction here?"

Hawker did. He said nothing.

The detective continued. "After our brief conversation on the telephone, I already knew you were familiar with police procedure—and that you were experienced enough not to be upset by the use of deadly force. Deduction: you were either a cop, a crook, or a police reporter. I took the liberty of running an NCIC check on you on the trip out. Results, I am happy to say, were negative—if you gave me your proper name. And if you didn't, we will find out soon enough. That left cop or reporter. I noticed your complicated-looking computer inside and, for a short time, I decided you were a reporter. But it's the rare reporter who can react quickly to armed assault. And I've yet to meet the reporter, thank God, who can make three perfect shots while under fire. Two in the kneecap, one through the brain. Final deduction: you, Mr. Hawker, are a cop. Or an ex-cop."

"Ex-cop," said Hawker. "Chicago."

"Chicago, is it? There's a fine city. Why did you quit?"

"Personal reasons." Hawker smiled. "But why ask? Tomorrow, when you get into the office, you'll make a phone call and have the Chicago department feed you a complete dossier."

Flaherty chuckled. "Why wait until tomorrow?" He checked his watch. "I don't go off duty for another two hours. Dreadful schedule, eh? Anyway, I suspect I'll have the information before sunrise." He flipped his notebook shut and stood as if to go.

"No questions about what happened?" asked Hawker, amused.

Flaherty shrugged. "Miss St. John gave me a very clear statement. If she was telling the truth, I have no doubt your story would only be repetitious. If she was lying, you two had sufficient time to make sure you both told the same story. That, too, would be repetitious. So, until we get some data on the dead man, there's little more to know. But you may be sure, Mr. Hawker, that I will be back if I have even the slightest suspicion that you killed the man for any reason other than self-defense."

"Never doubted it for a moment," said Hawker.

"Fine. Well, I'll be leaving, then, Mr. Hawker." Flaherty stopped to yawn in the doorway of the porch. "It's been a busy night for both of us."

"It has been that," said Hawker, suddenly alert. He sensed a trap.

Flaherty flashed a disarming smile. "Of course, you were more delightfully employed than I— spending the whole of the evening with the beautiful Miss St. John."

"I wish that were true. Unfortunately, Melanie didn't come by until very late."

"No? I could have sworn she told me she'd been with you all evening." He held up one finger again, nodding. "Well, now I remember—I guess I just *assumed* you had been together. It's the romantic in me. I pictured the sunset walk, the late dinner. My dear Irene wouldn't like it, of course, if I allowed myself to speculate further."

"Sorry to disappoint you, Lieutenant," Hawker said easily. "I spent most of the evening alone. I unplugged the phone and buried myself in computer books. It's a hobby of mine."

"Is that so? And not a single soul stopped by to bother you, I suppose?"

"Not until Melanie showed up. Of course, I was in bed by then."

"Of course, of course." Hawker felt the detective's prism eyes lock onto his. "Well, I am envious, Mr. Hawker. Quite envious. You could never guess how I spent the evening. Investigating more killings. Oh, it's an ugly business, police work. You were smart to get out of it. Yes, there's been a terrible rash of killings in the Starnsdale slums. Street gangs, you know. Like a pack of animals. They'd cut your throat for a dime. But lately only the gang members themselves have been getting themselves killed. Strange, eh?"

"We had a few street gangs in Chicago, Lieutenant. Nothing they did would surprise me."

"Oh? Well, you're right, I suppose. They're absolutely without scruples. The strange thing is, though, they usually blame the killings on another gang. But lately—you may find this interesting, Mr. Hawker—lately they've been blaming them on some mysterious red-haired man. Can you

imagine? They seem absolutely terrified of him.
After every killing he leaves his mark: the outline of a big bird of prey. An eagle, maybe"—
Flaherty's eyes bore into his—"or a hawk. Of
course, they're probably making it all up—con-
summate liars that they are. Even so, imagine my
surprise when I arrived to investigate the fourth
killing of the evening and found myself greeted by
a red-haired ex-policeman named Hawker."

"Quite a coincidence," said Hawker.

Flaherty nodded. He walked down the steps
into the yard before stopping. "Do you know what
the hardest thing about investigating those killings
is, Mr. Hawker?"

"I have a feeling you're going to tell me,
Lieutenant."

"The toughest thing is making myself *care*. I'm
sure, as an ex-policeman, you will understand.
Every street-gang member killed had a record as
long as your arm. They roam those slums like
rabid dogs. No human being in the area is safe as
long as they are allowed to go free. So I just don't
care if someone takes the risk of killing them. In
fact I'm rather glad because—as I'm sure you found
out—the courts are all too willing to see our hard-
earned arrests go free."

"It's frustrating," Hawker agreed mildly.

"Isn't it, though? Yes, I've often thought the
country would be much better off if the police
were allowed to punish certain criminals right at
the scene of the crime. Save the taxpayers so
much money. Yes, like all cops, I suppose, I occa-

sionally daydream about how nice it would be . . .
how *just* it would be . . . to occasionally take the
law into our own hands."

"Police work can push even honest cops to the
far right."

"Worse than that," said Lieutenant Detective
Flaherty. "Now I've got to hunt this mysterious
red-haired man down—this benefactor of citizen
and policeman alike—and see to it that he goes to
prison. Not a pleasant task, wouldn't you agree?"

"I don't envy you," said Hawker.

Flaherty pulled the hat down low over his ears
and studied the dark morning sky, as if looking for
rain. "Take care of yourself, Mr. James Hawker.
Walking a tightrope is a dangerous business at
best."

"I don't know what you're talking about," said
Hawker. "And I will."

thirteen

Hawker spent the next three days performing the innocent ceremonies of a man vacationing in California.

He was being followed. And he damn well knew it.

Hawker dutifully put in some dull afternoons as a tourist. His only satisfaction was in knowing that Flaherty would find it even more boring than he did.

The only things he did that were less than touristlike were to attend two Hillsboro watch meetings and the funeral of Julie Kahl.

The neighborhood watch meetings went without incident. Even the mountainous Sully McGraw seemed resigned to Hawker's leadership role—even though he was still less than friendly after the beating Hawker had given him. John Cranshaw said McGraw had decided to stay in the group because one of his pawnshops had recently been broken into—probably by street-gang hoods—and he was determined to get revenge.

The progress the group was making was impressive. The rape and murder of Virgil Kahl's daughter had unified the men as nothing else could. They worked with a brutal intensity toward one common goal: to throw off the shackles of fear which hobbled their community.

Julie Kahl's funeral was held on a summer-bright Monday morning. Hawker hated funerals, but he felt his presence was required. At Melanie St. John's insistence Hawker had given her a heavily edited account of his reasons for being in California. She was anything but dumb, and it was obvious he wasn't in L.A. looking for work. Hawker decided she deserved a more reasonable explanation, so he told her he was a private detective who was doing a favor for a friend. He said he had come out to investigate Julie Kahl's murder.

It was almost the truth, and Melanie accepted the story with a promise to help him if she could.

Hawker said she could start by going to the funeral with him. She agreed, and seemed to be as touched as Hawker by the number of teenagers and adults who came to pay their last respects.

Close to tears as they lowered the casket into the ground, Melanie had whispered in his ear, "Oh, James, I'm just realizing what a dirty town this is . . . and what an awful business I'm in."

"It could happen anywhere, Mel—and does.

And Julie Kahl had nothing to do with the film business. She was just another victim."

"But her father's in it . . . and I think I've seen her around the lot. . . . Oh, hell, I don't know what I mean. The business seems to be cursed with tragedy, and it seems to rub off on everyone. I've almost decided to quit, James. Maybe quit and move to some quiet midwestern town and marry some good man and raise fat babies."

Hawker felt her hand slip into his. He squeezed her hand and said nothing.

But aside from those two meetings and the funeral—all of which could be explained innocently—Hawker strictly played tourist.

The shrewdness of Lieutenant Walter Flaherty was not to be underestimated.

So he drove to Hollywood and matched handprints on the sidewalk of stars (and was surprised to find that Melanie had recently been immortalized there). He paid the admission price and toured Twentieth Century-Fox studios at Century City. He visited the Farmers Market, the La Brea tar pits, and took a bus tour of the homes of movie and television celebrities.

At Marina del Rey he lost Flaherty by strolling into the marina office, then running out the service entrance. He circled back to the black Ford and tapped Flaherty on the elbow.

"What? Oh!" Laughing, Flaherty touched his chest, startled. "What a turn you gave me."

"Just wanted to say good afternoon, Lieutenant."

"And a good afternoon to you, *Detective* Hawker."

Flaherty grinned. "You see, I did contact Chicago and get your dossier. And I must admit that I am impressed. Yes, indeed, quite impressed. I suspected you were a cop, but I had no idea you were one of the most decorated cops in Chicago's history. Medals for heroic service. Citations for bravery. Wounded twice in the line of duty. Founder of the Chicago SWAT team. Why, it's an honor to be following you."

"How'd you like the tar pits, Lieutenant?"

"Ah, all those poor animals. It fairly melts my heart to think of the poor dumb brutes sinking into the mire—even if it was a million years ago."

"I've got a soft spot for reptiles myself."

Flaherty held up an index finger in characteristic exclamation. "Two curious things have happened since I started following you, Detective Hawker."

"Oh, yeah?"

"Yes. And those curious things are: one, the killings in the Starnsdale slums have stopped; two, yesterday I received a package in the mail from an anonymous source.

"The package contained what appears to be a folder from someone's file. A very interesting file it is, too. Sloppily done, and hard to understand in some places, but it *seems* to be a record of illegal transactions by one of our beloved street gangs. Strange that a street gang would keep files, eh? It almost suggests some strong organizing force behind them, doesn't it?"

"Like I told you, nothing they did would surprise me—speaking from my experiences in Chicago, anyway." Hawker didn't add, of course, that he had sent Flaherty the file.

"Quite right, too," Flaherty agreed. "At any rate, this mysterious file mentions one very surprising name. Several times, in fact. It would be inappropriate for me to give the name to you— quiet, peace-loving vacationer that you are—but I will say that we are having the individual followed."

"Hope this person is enjoying it as much as I am."

"And one more bit of news, Detective Hawker. The man who broke into your cottage was a small-time drug dealer by the name of Conor Phelan. He was also suspected of being a PCP manufacturer. Angel dust. Ugly stuff that has turned more than one adolescent's brain to jelly."

"Conor Phelan? Sounds Irish, Lieutenant."

"A shame it is, too. And the rest of us have done so well as crooked union leaders and politicians—"

"And cops."

"Yes, and crooked cops, too." Flaherty checked his watch. "Will you be killing anyone for the next hour or so, Detective Hawker?"

"I don't have any immediate plans."

"What good news that is. I like to eat my lunch in peace."

The next day a different car followed Hawker. Hawker wondered if Flaherty was giving up, or if he just had something more important going.

It was his fourth day as a tourist, and he was getting antsy. He decided he could get a little work done under the guise of tourism, and maybe even rig it so he could slip out that night.

Hawker stopped at a custom T-shirt shop and drew the design he wanted on a piece of paper. The girl at the counter became instantly solicitous when he pulled two one-hundred-dollar bills out of his pocket and paid in advance.

Yes, sir, the shirts would be ready tomorrow. Yes, sir, they could certainly be delivered. Thank you, sir, and please call again.

Hawker had smiled and said he would—knowing full well he wouldn't.

His work was almost done in California. For that he was glad. He had come to associate the acid smell of Los Angeles with the profiteering stench of his enemy.

He would be glad to leave both far behind.

He would miss Melanie St. John. But he planned to get in touch with her later, maybe have her meet him in Chicago. Or Florida.

As he drove toward Hollywood, Hawker tested his own emotion electrodes, wondering how much he really felt for the actress. She had said that she loved him. But love, he had found, was a very cheap word in the film industry. As he drove, Hawker amused himself with the proper wording of another of his social truisms:

The instability of a given social sector can be effectively measured by its undisciplined use of emotional verbiage.

Maybe she did love him. Hawker doubted it— although it was clear she cared for him. But Hawker was even more troubled by the sudden knowledge that he cared more for her than he wanted to admit.

Hawker didn't want a woman now. Not a steady woman, anyway—however much his male ego was boosted by the knowledge that he had won the affection of one of the world's most beautiful film stars.

He had too much work to do to tie himself to a single female. He couldn't afford the emotional risks.

From now on, Hawker realized, women would be an indulgence. He would take them when he needed them. And then he would discard them.

His job required it.

Even if the woman was Melanie St. John.

Hawker shut out the thoughts as he turned into the World Film Studios lot. The guard stopped him at the main entrance.

"You got a pass, sir? You need to have a pass to get into the studios."

Hawker took out his billfold and flashed the tiny badge. Then he quickly put the billfold away so the guard wouldn't see that it was his badge from the Chicago P.D.

"Somebody here called and reported getting some obscene phone calls. I'm supposed to check it out."

The guard studied his clipboard again. "They

didn't call me to say you were coming. They're supposed to call."

Hawker shrugged. "Doesn't matter to me, buddy. These actor types are a pain in the ass, anyway. I'm just as happy if you don't let me in."

Hawker shifted the car into reverse, but the guard stopped him. "Naw, that's okay. Go on in. They'll get pissed off at me if you don't show."

"You must have some real bastards working in here."

The guard shook his head wearily. "You don't know the half of it, partner."

Hawker drove slowly past a line of buildings the size of jet hangars. A group of men in Indian costumes sat at a table outside playing cards and eating lunch. Gaffers pushed columns of lights on booms along the side of the road. Several men in business suits hurried after a striking blonde. Her T-shirt strained against her jiggling breasts.

The blonde glanced at Hawker, turned away, then glanced back and waved gaily. "Doug!" she exclaimed.

It was Trixie McCall. For some strange reason she looked younger and prettier in daylight.

Hawker waved back and drove on.

The personnel office was a small concrete-block building painted white. A window air conditioner rattled against the summer heat. Hawker walked up the steps and went in.

The woman at the desk looked as if she had spent her thirty-odd years eating nothing but cakes and cookies. The floor seemed to strain beneath the weight of her. Her yellow hair was piled on her head in a tight bun. The corpulent cheeks and jowls were interrupted by thin, tight lips and tiny little blue eyes.

"Yes?" The tone of her voice was chilly.

Hawker swung out the billfold. "Police. I'd like to take a quick look at one of your personnel files."

"Someone was already here. This morning. He had a warrant." The fierce little eyes challenged him. "Do you?"

"I'm working under the same warrant. He missed something. He sent me back."

"Lieutenant Flaherty?"

Hawker was both surprised and relieved. "Right."

The fat woman looked less than convinced. "So why don't you describe Flaherty for me?"

"You don't trust an honest cop?" Hawker gave her his best smile.

It didn't budge her. "There aren't any honest cops. Describe him, buddy."

Hawker described him. She seemed disappointed. The fat woman wheeled back in her chair with a heavy sigh, as if being forced to move ruined her whole day.

She pawed through a cabinet and tossed a file on the desk. "Make it quick," she said. "I've got work to do."

"I will—as soon as you bring me the right file."

"That's the one Flaherty wanted."

"That's why he sent me back. I need to check another one." Hawker leaned over the desk and scribbled the name on a piece of paper. "This is the one I want."

The woman looked puzzled. "I'll check to see if we have it—but I don't guarantee anything."

"You know," said Hawker. "Your cheeks get a nice color when you're mad. Kind of pretty."

The woman blushed. "You're just trying to get your file."

"That's right." Hawker grinned. "But that doesn't have anything to do with the way you look when you're mad."

She smiled for the first time. "Would I be helping you if I was mad?" she asked as she lumbered back to the cabinet.

fourteen

Hawker made one more stop—an appliance store—then drove back to his bungalow.

The wind blowing off the Pacific had a bite to it. The dusk sky was a luminous jade-green as the sun melted into the sea. The air smelled of rain.

From the wall phone in the kitchen Hawker watched the unmarked police car pull up to the beach and park.

Hawker checked his notebook and dialed. Virgil Kahl answered. Hawker had talked to him briefly at the funeral. He had looked twenty years older, a broken and beaten man.

Hawker didn't expect him to recover. He had lost too much. The listless voice on the other end confirmed Hawker's observations. Kahl sounded as if he was still in shock, far, far from the horrors of reality.

"James Hawker? Oh, yes—I remember. I saw you at the funeral, didn't I?"

"I've been working with the watch program, Virgil."

"Oh, yes, how could I have forgotten. This has been such a terrible, terrible week. We lost our daughter, you know. Our only child."

"I know, Virgil. And I'm sorry. That's why I called. I want you to do me a favor, Virgil."

"A favor? Certainly. I'd do anything for a friend of my daughter."

Hawker shook his head, feeling helpless. Kahl had gotten even worse. He decided to try, anyway. "Virgil, listen to me. I want to ask you a question. I need some information. Did you ever work with a young actor named Johnny Barberino? At World Film Studios, maybe?"

There was a long silence, as if he had to process each word individually. "Barberino? Why should I know him? I don't know any actors anymore."

"Are you sure, Virgil? Please think."

"I'm quite sure. Now, please don't bother me anymore. I'm tired of questions. We've lost our daughter, you know. Our . . . our only child."

The line suddenly went dead, and Hawker realized Kahl had hung up.

Feeling sickened by it all, Hawker cracked a cold bottle of Tuborg and took the Eavesdrop recorder onto the porch with him.

The talk in the Satanás' headquarters was the same as it had been for the last three days: speculation on who the Hawk was; wild talk of revenge and murder.

But this time the wild talk had crystallized.

Hawker listened closely as the recorder played back a telephone conversation for him. Hawker recognized both voices. The caller was Hammer, the half-breed leader of the Hispanic street gang. The other voice belonged to Razor, the Panthers' chieftain.

"You know who this is?" the tape began.

There was a long pause. "What the fuck you be callin' me for?"

"We got a problem, amigo. We got a *mutual* problem."

"Don't be giving me that 'amigo' shit, mother—"

"Razor, just calm down for a minute, man. You don't dig what I've got to say, just hang up. But at least listen."

"Make it quick, Hammer. The young dudes be getting real suspicious if they knew I'm talking to you."

"So shut up for a minute. Okay? Look, you've been getting burned by this Hawk dude, just like we have, right?"

"Until we kill the fucker—"

"You ain't killin' nobody, man! Face it. The fucker's too smart for you. He's been too smart for us, too—until now."

"What you mean, 'until now'?"

"I got a plan, Razor. But it's gonna take both groups. We're gonna have to have our boys hit together."

"Hit *who*? You think it gonna take thirty of us to kill this Hawk dude?"

"We're gonna hit the whole Hillsboro section, man. I've got some information from a good source. This Hawk is nothing but a jive ex-cop. He came to help them jerks in Hillsboro. Think about it, Razor. It makes sense. This fucker's been hired as a protector. If we send our dudes to Hillsboro, he's gonna show up. We'll march 'em right down the street, kicking ass the whole way. You and me and our main men will be waiting off to the side. When we catch the first glimpse of this red-haired character, we'll blow his ass away."

Razor chuckled. "Yeah? You're sure? Well, it may work. Smoke the motherfucker out."

"Damn right it'll work. I've already told my boys to meet at the corner of Hillsboro Boulevard tomorrow night. Midnight. I'm gonna start passing the word now that the Panthers are going to help us. And no fighting among ourselves, Razor. Tell that lunatic Amin to save it all for the Hawk."

"Yeah? Well, tell the same thing to them fucking weirdos of yours. That little crippled dude, Lobo, be screwin' kids, and that Jesús—"

"Hay-soos, dumb shit. It ain't pronounced 'gee-suz.' "

"I don't give a fuck how you spics say it. That Jesús cat gives me the heebie-jeebies."

"Just get the word to your boys, Razor. Get the word out today so they'll be ready. Just have them be at Hillsboro. Tell them to bring some tools— nothing heavy. Chains and canes. Tell 'em the plan and tell them to go heads up with the civilians. Remember, make it real clear you and me and our main men aren't exactly going to be leading them. We'll be off to the side, waiting for this Hawk to show."

"Midnight, right?"

"Right. And Razor—you and me and the other chiefs ought to get together tomorrow night before the hit and go over what we're going to do."

"Where?"

"Someplace neutral, man. You know where. The park. About ten."

"You bringing your three lieutenants, man?"

"Except Matador. He's got some business tomorrow night."

"Me and Amin and Blade will be there. And one more thing, Hammer."

"Yeah?"

"When we see this Hawk dude, we ain't gonna waste him. Not right there, anyway."

"No?"

"No." The tape recorder buzzed with Razor's oily laugh. "We gonna bring him back to the turf and have some fun, man. We're gonna do the same thing that fucker did to Cat Man. We're gonna to cut his dick off. And then I'm gonna add his little pink ears to my collection."

Hawker clicked off the recorder and reset it. Then he went to the phone and made two more calls.

The first was to John Cranshaw.

"How are the men doing, John?" Hawker asked after identifying himself.

"Great, James. Just great. I think they'll be ready for almost anything in another couple of weeks."

"They'll have to be ready a lot sooner than that."

"What?"

Hawker told him about the street gangs' plans. Cranshaw gave a low whistle. "Gee, I don't know, James. Maybe we'd better just call the police and let them handle it."

Hawker's voice turned cold. "Sure, John. Do that."

"It's just that it sounds dangerous."

"It will be. And it will be dangerous next week and the week after that. It will be dangerous just as long as they know they can bully you."

"But what if we . . . aren't ready?"

"It doesn't matter, John. All the men have to do is fight. And show they're not afraid."

Cranshaw cleared his throat nervously. Hawker waited as he thought it all out. Finally he said, "Damn it all, you're right! I'll call everyone tonight. It's time we stood and fought."

"You're making the right decision, John."

"Hell, I'm even looking forward to it." He chuckled. "It's going to feel good, acting like a man again."

"Personally, I don't think any of you ever stopped, John. By the way, some packages are going to be delivered to your house tomorrow. They're T-shirts. Have the men wear them."

"T-shirts?"

"Right. And one more thing, John—don't forget to call Sully McGraw. He's the kind of guy who likes to be reassured he's needed."

"He'll be first on the list. And, James? Thank you. Thank you for all your help."

Hawker hung up and then leafed through his notebook until he came to young Julio Castanada Balserio's name. The file he had stolen gave a telephone number but no address.

Hawker would have liked to see him in person, but he didn't have much time. Besides, Flaherty's man would have followed him.

An old woman answered on the first ring. In his kitchen Spanish, Hawker made it clear he wanted to speak with Julio.

There was a long wait while Julio's name was called loudly in the background.

"*Diga.*"

"Julio, this is a friend of yours. We met the other night—at the Satanás headquarters."

The young Latin was quiet for so long that Hawker began to wonder if he had fainted. Shifting to English, he finally said, "I got into a lot of trouble over that. They beat me. They beat me bad. I'm supposed to be in the hospital right now."

"They didn't beat you, Julio. They slapped you around. But they believed you. Save your lies for them, okay?"

"How . . . how did you know?"

"I know a lot of things, Julio. That's why I called you."

"I don't want to get into no more trouble."

"You won't. Not if you do exactly as I say."

"I'm listening."

"The Satanás and the Panthers are going to hit Hillsboro tomorrow night—together. Did you know that?"

Julio hesitated. "Yeah. Hammer called about an hour ago."

"He and the other leaders are going to meet in some park before the hit. I need to know which park, Julio."

"They didn't tell me, but I guess it would be Hyde Park. It's kinda weird, us two gangs getting together, but Hammer said there'd be nothing to it. Said the hit would be easy."

"That's bullshit, Julio. There's going to be a lot more to it than they think. Listen to me, Julio, and listen good. Hammer and the other leaders have been using you. You and all your friends. They let you guys do the dirty work while they sit back and collect the profits."

"What profits, man?"

"What do you think they do with that stuff they have you steal?"

"We don't do no stealing."

"I've seen your headquarters, remember, Julio?"

"Well, I guess we do steal. Some. But Hammer don't cheat us. He uses the money to fix up the headquarters. He bought us jackets."

"There were enough stolen stereos and television sets alone to buy a new headquarters, Julio. Use your head for a second. He fences that stuff to professionals, and he and his four sick friends split the money. They give you guys just enough to keep you happy. And it's not hard to keep you happy because they keep pounding that 'die-for-the-Satanás' crap into your heads. They use the money they make to buy drugs. The drugs they don't use, they sell. They're getting fat, and they're laughing at you guys behind your backs."

"I kinda wondered why they didn't make more money off the TVs and stuff," Julio admitted grudgingly. "But why's it so important that you got to tell me?"

"Because I want you tell the others. Tomorrow, when you get to the corner of Hillsboro, tell them what I've just told you. Tell them they're being made fools of. And one way or another they're going to end up paying with their lives. In a prison cell or a coffin. Tell them that."

"In front of Hammer? He *would* beat me then."

"Hammer's not going to be there. Not out in the open, anyway. And neither are any of the other leaders. They're going to let you guys take the heat. And I'm hoping you're too smart to get burned, Julio. Think it over."

"Yeah," he said. "Yeah, I guess I will."

"And, Julio—don't double-cross me. Don't think you can save yourself by going to Hammer tonight and telling him what I said."

The laughter was edged with star-struck surprise. "Double-cross the Hawk, man? You think I'm *nuts*? I still ain't convinced I'm not talking to the devil right now. . . ."

fifteen

The street-gang chieftains were supposed to meet at Hyde Park at ten P.M.

Hawker was there by nine.

For the second day in a row Flaherty left Hawker's tail to another officer. It gave Hawker more confidence in his escape plan. He used the electric time switch he had bought at the appliance store to turn the bungalow's stereo and lights on and off.

At eight thirty the stereo and the living-room lights would go on. At eleven both would switch off and the bathroom light would come on. It would stay on for ten minutes.

In the mind of the cop parked outside, Hawker would be spending another leisurely evening at home.

He would be wrong, of course.

At first dusk Hawker slid out the side window. He carried his equipment in a canvas duffel bag.

He jogged east toward the light and noise of Sepulveda Boulevard. When Hawker was sure Flaherty's man had not followed him, he hailed a cab. He gave the driver a fake address in Willowbrook, a suburb not far from Hillsboro. When Hawker judged they were near Hyde Park, he told the driver to stop. He said he wanted to walk the rest of the way.

Hyde Park was a cool mound of trees and rolling lawn in the slum sprawl near Starnsdale. There was playground equipment illuminated by the cold glare of vapor lights. Swings moved languidly on their chains in the Pacific wind.

Hawker made a casual trip through the park. Midway through was a wide fountain with running water. Underwater lights illuminated the fountain, but the overhead vapor light had been broken— shot out, probably.

It looked like a probable meeting place.

Hawker continued on to the south edge of the park. Except for a couple of winos sleeping on street-side benches, the place was deserted.

Hawker returned to the fountain, studying the heavy oak trees that surrounded it. Over one thick limb he tossed a grappling hook, then tested it with his full weight. Carrying the bitter end of the rope, Hawker climbed high into the branches of another tree.

Hawker knew he might have to move—and move quickly.

The rope would help.

He pulled the rope tight. If they noticed it at all, it would look like a power cable.

Straddling a limb, Hawker braced his back comfortably against the tree. From the pack he took a cut-down version of the Cobra crossbow. It was made of light, alloy metal and had a heavy woven drawcord. By breaking the crossbow over his knee, he caused the self-cocking device to lock the hundred-pound pull drawcord in place.

The Cobra had a killing range of two hundred meters. The short aluminum shafts—or bolts—traveled a hundred yards a second.

Hawker inserted a three-edge kill bolt and rested the crossbow on his knee.

It was nine twenty P.M.

He waited.

The Panther chieftains arrived half an hour later. Razor came sliding through the shadows, whistling softly. His hands were in his pockets, as if he were out for an evening stroll. The earring glinted in the lobe of his ear.

He made a relaxed trip around the fountain perimeter, his quick eyes surveying the area. When he was sure it was safe, he waved his two lieutenants in.

Amin was dressed in the same clothes he'd worn when Hawker first saw him. The chain was still belted around his huge waist. His belly protruded from the open Levi's jacket. His black boots glistened and his massive biceps flattened themselves against his sides.

Blade came next. His wild Afro haircut waved in the wind like a headdress. A cigarette hung from the corner of his mouth. There was a distant, dreamy look in his eyes as he mechanically opened and closed his switchblade. Hawker guessed he had recently shot up.

"They ain't here yet," Razor said.

Amin looked nervous. His massive, black gorilla face tracked back and forth, like a radar dish. "Don't like it, man. Don't like this joint operation shit."

"We done it before. Can't operate without the Hammer. He got the connections."

"Yeah, but we never done it without the soldiers. What if they catch on, man? They put two and two together, and we out of business."

"Them boys ain't gonna put nothing together."

"Still don't like it, Razor. We ain't never let the soldiers mix alone before."

"And we never had this Hawk dude sneaking around killin' us before, either, Amin. Just relax, man. Relax."

"What if Hammer set us up? What if he brought us here to hit us?"

Razor shook his head, getting weary of the conversation. "He needs us, too, man. If it's a trap, I'll recognize it."

"Then what?"

"Then we kill *them* first. You carrying?"

Amin patted the bulge beneath his jacket. "Got a .44 Magnum. Blow their fucking Spanish asses away, they mess with Amin."

Blade chuckled as if in approval. He said nothing. Hawker noted the bulge beneath his jacket.

They were all armed.

A few minutes later Hammer arrived. He was backed by the wolfish sexual deviant, Lobo, and Jesús, the self-styled prophet. Hawker noted that Matador, the suave drug addict, wasn't with them. He wondered if he might be somewhere in the bushes, gun ready.

It was not a friendly group.

The animosity and distrust among the four lieutenants was like a sour odor in the air. They glared at each other, playing stare-down like kids.

Hammer ignored it. He pawed at his nose like a boxer and spat. "We got problems," he began.

Razor stiffened. "You said it was smooth, man. You said it was all set."

"That was last night. My connection's upset about something. He's going to meet us here. He wouldn't talk on the phone. He's late."

Razor jammed his fists on his hips. "Don't be fucking with us, Hammer! You pull any shit with us—"

"Calm down, damn it!" Hammer snapped. "You think I want trouble, man? All I want is a clean operation. If my connection says we got trouble, then we gotta listen. He wants to make his money, too, and he knows if he ain't straight, then we go someplace else."

Jesús crouched suddenly. "Someone's coming, man!"

"It's him," said Hammer. "Relax."

Razor waved Amin and Blade back into the bushes. "If this dude's as straight as you say he is, then you won't mind if we just sort of disappear for a minute, will you?" Razor said, testing.

"I don't give a fuck what you do," Hammer snapped.

The footsteps were getting closer—a big man not used to moving quietly. Twigs broke beneath him, and the breathing was heavy.

Hawker was not surprised to see who walked into the dim glow of the fountain.

The man Hammer referred to as his "connection" was huge. His face was red, visibly agitated. He wore black slacks and a straw-colored Cuban shirt. He took a cigarette and lighted it before he spoke.

Hawker noticed that the man's hands shook slightly as he held the lighter.

It was Sully McGraw.

"I couldn't talk on the phone," McGraw said without preamble. "That bastard's got a tap on. Has to."

Hammer's face was like rock. "You could have called from a pay phone, McGraw. You can't tap every pay phone in Starnsdale."

"It's not my phone that's tapped, dumb shit," McGraw said, exhaling smoke. "It's yours. How else do you figure Hawker knew about your hit tonight? Christ, he called Cranshaw—the watch group's leader. Told him all about your plans. Told him what time, where, and how many to expect. The bastards are laying for you. They're ready."

"How you know that, man?" demanded Razor as his men followed him out of the bushes.

"You're with the Panthers?"

"Yeah."

"Then he's probably got a tap on you, too. It's a guy named Hawker. A red-haired guy. Says he's an ex-cop, but I think he's with the feds. I joined the watch group a year ago to sort of keep an eye on things. When Hawker showed up, I smelled something rotten. The fucker's smart. Too smart. When I started reading in the paper about your people getting bumped off, it all started to make sense."

"You think he knows about the fencing operation?" Hammer asked. "Because if he knows, we might as well pack—"

"I'm already cashed in and packed," interrupted McGraw. "Believe me, I wouldn't leave a chain of pawnshops and a hundred-thousand-dollar house behind if I didn't think my ass was on the line—"

"Wait a minute," Hammer cut in, his face grown suddenly pale. "If he knows about our plans for the hit tonight, then—"

"Then he probably knows about us meeting right now," Razor finished, drawing a revolver from his jacket.

In a moment they all had guns out—including McGraw. Hawker drew back into the shadows of the tree as their eyes darted back and forth, searching the cover. As they looked, the seven men backed into a loose circle.

Lobo was the first to notice the rope. Hawker

watched him closely. He watched the pale, wolfish eyes following the rope. As Hawker watched, he thought about Lobo's police record. Sexual deviant. Child molester. Hawker wondered how many terrified kids had looked into those sick, sick eyes.

Lobo's eyes peered deeply into the shadows of the tree. Hawker drew back, holding perfectly still. Lobo started suddenly, and his eyes grew wide. His gun jumped toward Hawker, and his mouth opened as if to shout out a warning.

But the words never came.

Hawker lifted the modified Cobra and squeezed the trigger.

All the other men heard was a whistle of air and a thud. Lobo jolted to the ground, his hands scratching at his chest.

His mouth was still open as if to shout. Bloody bubbles formed on his lips. He studied the stub of plastic feathers which protruded from his chest, as if perplexed.

He died with the look of confusion frozen on his face.

"Son of a bitch!" shouted Razor as he and the others slowly realized what had happened. "Where in the fuck is he?"

"Over there!"

"Naw, it had to come from over *there*!"

They flattened themselves on the ground, guns firing wildly into the bushes.

"Wait a minute!" yelled McGraw. "He's up there. In the tree!"

From his weapons cache Hawker had taken another Ingram. This one didn't have a silencer, but it no longer mattered. He grabbed the end of the rope and swung away toward the fountain.

A salvo of lead cracked branches behind him.

With the fountain between him and the others Hawker released the rope as he crashed through a wedge of bushes. He dived for the protection of the fountain's rock retainer and came up firing.

The chain-rattle bursts from the Ingram roared in his ears, the barrel hot in his left hand.

Hammer and Razor were standing side by side. Hawker swung the Ingram at them, as if making sweeping brushstrokes.

Hammer screamed and clawed at his throat. As Razor turned to look, his cheek exploded. The impact of slug against bone snapped Razor's head back, breaking his neck, and he collapsed to the ground as if he had been magically deboned.

Hammer writhed on the earth beside him, bleeding from two black holes in his neck.

With the same drug-dazed expression Jesús charged Hawker, the revolver in his hand spitting fire. The slugs smacked into the water inches from Hawker's head.

Hawker swiveled and squeezed off four shots in rapid fire. Jesús jerked backward as if absorbing a series of blows, spinning wildly. The fountain retainer caught him thigh-high, and he fell face first into the water.

The lighted spray began to glow red.

"You *dead*, motherfucker!"

It was Blade. Hawker hadn't noticed Blade

circling around behind him. Hawker pivoted toward the voice just as Blade leaped toward him, the switchblade making a silver arc toward his face.

Hawker ducked to the side, then cracked down hard on Blade's elbow with the metal butt of the Ingram.

Dug addict or not, Blade was quick. From his knees he grabbed the submachine gun, trying to wrestle it away. Hawker kicked him in the stomach twice, hard. When Blade released the weapon, Hawker locked his right fist on the black man's throat. He jerked up and away with all his force.

Clutching his ruined neck, Blade rolled over and over, his feet kicking wildly, his eyes bulging.

Something hit Hawker from behind. It was like being hit by a truck. He was being driven toward the rock retainer wall of the fountain. Something hard and cold was locked around his neck. Hawker forced his fingers under it, trying to stop the crushing weight on his throat.

It was a chain.

Amin's chain.

Amin was trying to ram him into the rock wall before finally choking him to death.

The wall rushed toward Hawker. His head roared from lack of oxygen. He punched backward, driving his elbow deep into Amin's stomach.

Amin didn't seem to notice.

Just as his face was about to smash into the wall, Hawker made a last-ditch effort. He dropped to one knee and thrust forward with his upper body.

The momentum carried Amin over him. The chain jerked violently away from his neck as the huge man tumbled into the knee-deep water.

Hawker threw himself onto Amin's massive shoulders and used his elbow like an axe, to chop down hard on the back of his neck.

Amin bellowed like a wounded animal. They were both in the water now. Amin struggled to his feet and swung a giant right fist at Hawker's head. Hawker caught most of it with his forearm, but the force of the punch still knocked him down.

Amin lunged at him, but Hawker rolled away. They both floundered to their feet, but Hawker was a step faster. He launched a sizzling left hook into the big man's ribs, then followed with three quick rights that cracked Amin's face open.

From somewhere a knife appeared in Amin's hand. Hawker clubbed him once more in the face, then tripped his legs from under him. As he went down face first, Hawker locked his hands on the back of Amin's neck, holding the grotesque face underwater.

Amin struggled savagely for half a minute, then drew still.

Hawker let the corpse drift away as he climbed wearily to his feet.

"Impressive, Hawker," said a voice. "Damned impressive. You killed six out of seven. But six out of seven isn't good enough in a game like this. Now you're going to die."

Hawker turned to see Sully McGraw standing a

few feet away, his revolver beaded on Hawker's chest.

"You make me sick, McGraw."

The fat man allowed a thin smile to cross his lips. "Because I double-crossed my fine, upstanding neighbors? Tsk, tsk. Or because my business partners are"—his eyes surveyed the carnage meaningfully—"I should say *were* drug addicts and criminals? Either way it doesn't bother me, Hawker. My neighbors in Hillsboro are fools. And these dead lunatics made me a lot of money. They stole cheap. And I sold expensive."

"So now you're a rich and happy man," Hawker said with heavy sarcasm. "How long did it go on, McGraw?"

"From the moment I got smart and decided the life of the poor but honest businessman was for schmucks. Owning a pawnshop, I got plenty of hot stuff offered to me. So, about four years ago, I started going for it. Built up a nice little organization. The more money I made, the more shops I bought. Every now and then I'd stage a fake break-in just to keep the cops from getting suspicious. It was going real smooth until you showed up, Hawker." McGraw drew back the hammer of the revolver.

Hawker's mind raced, looking for some opening. McGraw was about ten feet away from him—too far to try to jump him. And the knee-deep water would make any running impossibly slow. Hawker kept talking, fighting for time. "And what about your drug connections, McGraw?"

He shrugged. "What this scum did with their money was no skin off my nose. If they wanted to buy and sell drugs, that was their business."

"But you knew about their Hollywood connection?"

"Julie Kahl, you mean? She was just a dumb little mixed-up girl. Wanted to be a star, and her daddy didn't have the pull anymore. So she tried to worm her way in with the drugs. Virgil suspected, but he never had the balls to do anything about it. But she was strictly nickel-and-dime stuff." McGraw's thin smile grew wicked. "America would crap its pants if Hollywood's main drug connection was ever caught. But you'll never have a chance to find out, Hawker, because I'm tired of talking. And I'm tired of looking at that ugly broken nose of yours." He gripped the gun in both hands. "Have a nice trip to hell, Hawker—"

"I'd be dropping the gun, if I were you," interrupted a voice from the shadows, "unless you're interested in making the same journey."

McGraw's face went white. He hesitated as if about to drop his gun, but then he pivoted and began to fire wildly toward the trees.

A deeper *ker-whack* erupted twice from the bushes. Sully McGraw buckled over as the slugs slammed him backward.

McGraw gasped as he struggled to turn his revolver toward Hawker. Hawker watched with a mild and distant interest as McGraw died with his eyes open, glaring at the California night sky.

"Nice shooting," Hawker said to the voice's unseen owner.

"Coming from you, that's a high compliment indeed."

Holding a .44 automatic, Lieutenant Detective Walter Flaherty materialized from the shadows.

sixteen

"Good evening, Detective Hawker."

Hawker stepped out of the fountain and inspected McGraw's body. "I never thought I'd be saying this, but I'm damn glad to see you, Lieutenant."

"Ah, sure, and I'm growing rather fond of you myself." Flaherty walked around the fountain, touching bodies with the toe of his brown shoes. "The lawyers aren't going to make a cent off these lads, are they?"

"How did you find me? How did you know where I'd be?"

Flaherty sniffed and blew his nose. He was wearing a gray tweed jacket and baggy pants. He stuffed the handkerchief into his back pocket. "The marvelous recording machine back at your little cottage told me. Interesting conversations those

Panthers and Satanás had. They do have the poet's
touch with profanity, don't they? I cringe to think
how my dear Irene would react if she heard such
talk." Flaherty smiled. "When they said they would
meet at a neutral park, I immediately knew it
would be Hyde Park." He winked. "I know the
territory, you see. And I've also come to know
you. I suspected you would be here."

"You broke into my place? You had a warrant, I
suppose."

Flaherty's face created a mock look of chagrin.
"Ummm . . . I did not. And I'm rather ashamed.
Are you going to tell?"

"I don't think it'd be much of a bargaining tool
with the Los Angeles district attorney."

"What? No, I suppose not—upstanding man that
he is. Wouldn't carry much weight at all, I'm
afraid."

"You decoyed me, Flaherty. You put another
man on as my tail. I should have known. He was
just a front, wasn't he?"

"Not at all, not at all—do you think I'm a sneak?"
Flaherty looked offended. "I found the files you
sent very interesting. It didn't tell me anything I
didn't already suspect, but it gave me sufficient
leverage for a fine and proper arrest warrant. It is,
in fact, the very reason I stopped by your cottage.
I was going to honor you with an invitation to
come along." He shrugged. "Obviously that was
impossible, since you weren't there. I gave the
detective who was supposed to be watching you a

regular tongue lashing, I did—then sent him and two other men to make the collar by themselves."

"Johnny Barberino."

"Of course." Flaherty pulled his jacket open and holstered the .45 as he sat on the fountain's rock ledge. "I actually owe you a great debt, James. I'd been trying to break this ring for the last five months. Of course, I knew most of the particulars, but, as you well know, getting court-worthy evidence is sometimes a difficult matter. You shook things up. You created in them the proper atmosphere of chaos—and chaos begets mistakes. Barberino assigned the poor lad with the red beard, Conor Phelan, to kill you. That was a mistake. McGraw there, rest his evil soul, began liquidating some of his properties—properties with value all out of proportion to his legal income. That was another mistake. And then I got a call from a rather plump blond secretary at World Film Studios—"

"But you'd already been there."

Flaherty held up one finger in characteristic exclamation. "Yes, but I went to see Johnny Barberino's file—not Julie Kahl's. I was as surprised as you may have been to discover that last summer while she was on vacation, she worked as an extra on one of Barberino's films." Flaherty meshed his hands together. "It all fit. The street gangs. Julie Kahl's murder. Sully McGraw. And Barberino." Flaherty chuckled. "And do you know why the secretary called me? She had failed to get your name. You were just a bit too charming, James. The young lady wanted to see you again."

"Great," said Hawker ruefully. He stood. "So now you read me my rights and take me in?"

Flaherty ignored him and held out his hand, palm up. "Ah, it's a fine, soft night, isn't it? Maybe just a touch of rain in the air." He looked at Hawker. "I'm out for my evening stroll, you see. It's not my night to work." He considered the sky again. "Yes, indeed, a lovely evening."

"A cop is always on duty. You're an agent of the court, even when you're off duty."

Flaherty snapped his fingers. "I've erred again, blast it! What you say is true, of course. Just like the search warrant business. I really must sit down with all the rules and regulations one afternoon and give them a thorough read. These mistakes will be the end of a struggling career, if I'm not careful."

His prism eyes lasered into Hawker's. "But as it stands now, Detective Hawker, you are a free man. I've yet to see you kill anyone, and if you've been as careful here as you've been in the past, you've left no prints, no registered weapons that can be traced to you . . . nothing at all but circumstantial evidence. And frankly, you've probably saved a fair number of innocent lives—not to mention suffering and taxpayers' money—in killing those you did. They will not be missed. Indeed, we are better off without them."

Hawker studied the little man before him for a time in silence. Finally he nodded. "I've met a lot of cops and a lot of detectives in my career, Walter. And if they were all after me at once, you're the only one I would really be worried about."

"Ha! Well, that is flattering. And if it's true, then I suggest you take the morning plane for Chicago. Because tomorrow afternoon I will come after you, Detective Hawker. And, as much as I'd hate it, I'm afraid I'd be forced to take you to prison."

Flaherty stood and took Hawker's outstretched hand.

Humming a strange little tune then, he strolled off into the shadows of Hyde Park. Hawker watched until he was gone, then began to collect his gear.

seventeen

At one A.M. Hawker telephoned John Cranshaw.

Hawker's single bag was packed, and he had readied the two crates of weaponry—and another crate with his computer—for pickup by an express freight carrier and shipment back to Chicago.

There was a seven A.M. flight to O'Hare, and Hawker planned to be on it.

Cranshaw answered on the second ring.

"James! You should have been there! Where the hell were you? It was great—"

"Calm down, John." Hawker laughed. Cranshaw's enthusiasm already told Hawker what he wanted to know—but he listened anyway.

"James, it was perfect!" Cranshaw chuckled. "We met just like you told us, and we put on those T-shirts you ordered. There were about twenty of us, and everybody was bitching and moaning about having to wear these stupid shirts—but we were all really just trying to cover up how damn scared we were."

"I don't blame you," Hawker put in.

"So we marched right down Hillsboro Boulevard. We could see those bastards waiting for us—both street gangs, the Panthers *and* the Satanás. Hell, there must have been forty of them.

"But the men were great, James. Stuck right to formation, just like you trained us. We got closer, and closer, and damned if we couldn't see their expressions change. The bastards were scared, James! Half of the youngest members just turned tail and ran. Some little Hispanic kid led them away, yelling something about hawks. I mean, it was like those black T-shirts with the big white bird head on the front just scared the crap out of them. Can you imagine? Why in the hell would that scare them, James?"

"It's a mystery to me," said Hawker. "I just thought it would be nice if you had a sort of uniform."

"Well, those T-shirts are our uniforms now, you can bet on that. There were about twenty gang members left, and we went right through them with that wedge formation. Then we broke into our five-man teams and went to work. Hell, those hoods were so confused and scared it didn't last more than five minutes. They ran like scared rabbits. I'll tell you, James, you've never seen so many proud middle-aged men in your life. We've got our neighborhood back, James. And for the first time in a long while, we've got our pride. . . ."

The two men talked for a while longer as Cranshaw discussed specifics, described small problems that would be fixed in the future, and lingered over funny anecdotes. He finally let Hawker hang up—but only after he had promised to return someday to Los Angeles.

Hawker wondered if he really would.

From the refrigerator he took a fine and bitter Guinness and popped it open. He found stationery and composed a note. It was his final goodbye—a farewell to Melanie St. John.

The desk was littered with crumpled paper by the time he had a paragraph that was satisfactory. That done, he took a long hot shower, opened another beer, then walked barefooted through the sand and the shadows toward the beach-side mansion built high in the trees.

A balmy wind blew off the Pacific. Far out on the horizon Hawker could see the faint lights of a freighter. They twinkled in the rolling darkness like stars.

Hawker walked up the asphalt drive. There were lights on in the house, and as he got closer he could see that someone was sitting on a deck chair on the broad, open porch.

It was Melanie.

Hawker's plan had been to tack the note to the door, return to his cottage, and get a few hours of much-needed sleep before catching his plane.

But it was too late for that. Her voice called out softly, "James? James, is that you?"

"Just wanted to leave you a note. I'm leaving in the morning, and I just wanted to say—"

"Wait. Don't go yet. I'll be right down."

She wore a white satinlike jogging suit. The jacket was half open in front, and he could see she wore no clothes beneath it. She came out the front door and hugged him warmly. In the dim light he could see that she had been crying.

"What's the matter, Mel?"

She shook her head, trying to gain control of herself. "I got a call about an hour ago. It was Johnny."

"Barberino?"

"Yes. He . . . he was arrested tonight. One of his weird friends was with him—some guy who called himself Matador. He tried to put up a fight when the police came, and they shot him. He's dead. Johnny said it was awful. He said he'd never seen anything like that, and it made him realize what a . . . what a fool he'd been. He was arrested for drug trafficking, James."

Hawker stopped himself in time from saying, "I know."

Melanie locked her arms across her chest and leaned her head on his shoulder. "He said he needs me, James. He wants me to come down tonight. To the jail."

"Oh?"

"I've spent the last hour wondering what in the

hell I should do. I loved him once . . . in a way. Maybe even more than I wanted to admit."

"I know the feeling."

She looked up at him, her eyes glistening. "Do you? Oh, I would feel so much better knowing that. Because . . . because I'm going to go, James. It sounds like he wants to change, James. And if that's true . . ."

Hawker took her shoulders gently and held her away from him. "You'll never know for sure unless you give him a chance, Mel."

She sighed and sagged against him. She took his face in her hands and kissed him tenderly, stroking the back of his neck. "If it doesn't work out, James—"

"If it doesn't work out, give me a call." Hawker grinned. "Maybe you could even visit me in Chicago."

She wiped her eyes, smiling for the first time. "Why do you have to be so damn nice? This would be a hell of a lot easier if you yelled and screamed and told me what a stupid bitch I'm being."

Hawker turned her and slapped her on the fanny. "Go see your man, lady. You'll both feel better."

"And I *am* going to visit you in Chicago!"

"Call first. I'll want to clean the bathtub."

Hawker watched her disappear into the house— and out of his life—before walking back toward his cottage. He stopped on the beach for a few minutes and threw rocks toward Hawaii, wondering why pretty, intelligent women so often dedicated themselves to spoiled men-children.

Johnny Barberino was a lucky man. Hawker wondered if he would ever know it.

Tired of feeling sorry for himself, Hawker jogged over the dunes and back to his bungalow. The lights were off. He stopped, trying to remember if he had left them on.

He was almost sure that he hadn't.

Carefully and quietly he nudged the front door open. He carried no weapon, so he kept his right hand squeezed tight in a fist as he made his way through the darkness.

"Yoo, hoo, is that you, Doug?" called out a high, squeaky voice.

Hawker flicked on the living-room light. Through the open bedroom door he could see the unmistakable shape of Trixie McCall beneath the white sheet of his double bed.

She grinned and waved at him. "I have been looking and *looking* for you, Doug. That day I saw you at the studio I broke a heel running after your car. Turned my ankle and couldn't even walk for an hour. People thought I was nuts."

Hawker switched on the desk light in the bedroom. "Look, Trixie, I'm flattered and all, but I really don't think—"

She swung the sheet away, revealing what Hawker suspected—she wore nothing but an ankle bracelet. "Oh, Doug, please don't be mean to me tonight," she purred. "I'm being as open as I can with you."

"I can see that."

She slid off the bed and came to him. Her nipples were large and erect on her firm breasts, and the hair on her thigh confirmed that she was, indeed, a natural blonde. She wrapped her arms around him and kissed his ear. "You're so masculine, Doug, like a real, live man—"

"Trixie, don't."

"And you've got such broad shoulders, and I like that funny, humpy nose—"

Her fingers had found his belt. "Trixie, I've got a plane to catch in the morning. I've got to get some sleep."

There was the sound of a zipper, and Hawker discovered that his traitor hands were exploring the glories of her body. "Ummm . . ." she whispered as his pants slid away. "No one sleeps in Los Angeles, silly."

"I'm beginning to believe that," said James Hawker as he lifted the naked woman into his arms and carried her toward the bed. . . .

Coming soon!

HAWKER #3

CHICAGO ASSAULT

two

Hawker grabbed Felicia by the shoulders and swung her away just before her husband was hit.

Her face was frozen in shock. "My God," she whispered. "My God . . . that was . . . that was . . . *Saul!*"

His name escaped her lips in a low wail.

Hawker pulled her inside. He fumbled for the switch and the overhead neons blinked on. There were shouts of drunken protest from the naked people on the floor. The black girl was still on the couch. Hawker grabbed her by the arm and jerked her away from the man who had mounted her.

"Get your hands off me, man. You got no right—"

Hawker shook her roughly. "Shut up," he said in an even voice. "Shut up and listen. Get some clothes on. Find some brandy. Then take Mrs.

Beckerman to the bedroom. Don't let her go near that balcony, understand?"

Hawker didn't wait for a response. The man who had been with the black girl was in his mid-fifties. He had neatly trimmed silver hair and was in surprisingly good shape. He looked as if he was probably respectable and reliable under different circumstances. Hawker grabbed him by the arm. "Are you sober enough to take charge here?"

"Hey—what . . . Yes, of course—"

"Then get these people out of here. Mr. Beckerman's been murdered. Call the police as soon as you can."

"Murdered? My God—"

Hawker shoved his way through the living room and out the double doors. As he sprinted down the hall he drew the customized Colt Commander .45 from the shoulder holster beneath his jacket.

The elevator was not in use. Hawker ignored it. He threw open the door of the stairwell and ran down the steps three at a time.

He stepped carefully into the hallway on the nineteenth floor. He could hear the low sound of voices. Anxious voices. Hawker moved toward the suite beneath Beckerman's apartment.

The door was cracked open. The voices came from inside.

Hawker hugged the wall as he moved toward the room. When he was about ten yards away two figures bolted from the room. Two white males in their late twenties or early thirties.

One was holstering a revolver beneath his gray

sport jacket as he ran. The other carried an ugly little automatic in his left hand.

"Freeze!" Hawker held the Colt Commander in both hands, level and ready, as he yelled.

The man with the automatic spun, his eyes wide with surprise. He burst off three wild shots. The automatic popped with the sound of books slapping together. The third shot ricocheted off the wall above Hawker.

Hawker squeezed off one careful round. In the narrow confines of the hallway the explosion was deafening.

The slow .45 slug smacked through the man's chest and sent him skidding backward, as if on ice.

Blood coated the white marble floor.

"Get your hands against the wall," Hawker yelled. The second man was frozen near the elevator, right hand inside his jacket. "Move!" Hawker commanded. "Hands against the wall—now!"

Slowly the man turned toward the wall, hands high. Hawker stalked toward him. The man had black curly hair and the damaged, aged face of a drug user or an alcoholic. He kept glancing over his shoulder at Hawker—or at the apartment where they had just killed Saul Beckerman.

Hawker kicked the man's feet wider. "Nose to the wall, asshole," he said evenly.

"You a cop?" the man demanded.

"No. But I'm the guy who's going blow your ears off if you so much as sneeze."

"You got no right to be doing this, man. You're no cop. You got no right—"

Hawker smacked him in the back of the head. The impact knocked the man's nose against the wall, and his nose began to bleed.

"*Shit!*" the man hissed.

"Idle talk makes me real grumpy," Hawker snapped. "Keep it in mind. That's why you're going to tell me why you killed Beckerman. You're going to tell me first, and then you're going to tell the cops—"

"I hardly think so," interrupted a strange voice from behind Hawker. Hawker's head swung around. The door to the apartment had been quietly pulled open. A squat, broad-shouldered man with a beefy red face stood in the doorway holding a Smith & Wesson Air Weight .38.

"Kindly toss your gun away," the man commanded. "*Now.*"

Hawker bent and placed the Colt on the floor near his feet.

"Now kick it away, like a good lad."

The man had a light Irish accent. But there was the calm edge of the trained killer in his voice too.

Hawker kicked the gun away.

"Christ, Kevin," whined the man with the bloody nose, "what took you so long?"

"Just straightening up inside the apartment. It pays to be careful, don't you see. Billy's dead?"

The man with the bloody nose retrieved his automatic and turned toward Hawker. "Yeah. This son of a bitch blew him away." He pointed the gun at Hawker's head. "Now I'm going to kill you, you bastard."

"By all means," said Kevin calmly. "Make it quick, lad. We've still got to find a back way out of here and meet our pickup."

"But first I'm going to bust his nose," said the kid, "just like he busted mine."

It was a mistake. Hawker knew it, and at once felt some hope of escape. The Irishman, Kevin, knew it, too, and he tried to stop the kid.

"Don't hit him, you stupid fool! Just shoot him and be done with it—"

The kid lowered his weapon and threw an overhand right at Hawker's face. Hawker stepped under the punch and slammed his fist deep into the kid's solar plexus.

The kid made a whoofing sound as Hawker swung him toward the Irishman. The two men collided in a tangle of arms and legs.

Hawker dove for his Colt Commander. Two slugs exploded off the floor beside his head.

Hawker's right hand found the cold weight of his weapon, and he rolled onto his back, firing four rounds in rapid succession.

The kid was slammed backward into the wall. His little automatic spun wildly in the air as his face melted into black gore.

The Irishman clutched the spreading stain on his jacket as if trying to stop a leak. His .38 fell from a quivering index finger as he slid down the wall.

Hawker got to his feet and went to the Irishman.

He was dying, and he knew he was dying. A helpless smile crossed his pale face. "The stupid kid," he whispered. "A stupid opening to give you."

"Yeah," said Hawker. "It was pretty dumb." He knelt beside the dying man. "Why did you do it?" he demanded. "Why did you kill Beckerman?"

The Irishman studied in disbelief the blood seeping from between his fingers, then looked at Hawker. "Orders, of course. We had orders."

"Whose orders, dammit? Who would have you hit a guy like Beckerman?"

Blood bubbled from the Irishman's lips with the soft chuckle. "And why would I be telling the man who . . . who killed me?"

His head slumped sideways, eyes frozen wide.

He was dead.

The hydraulic whine of the elevator told Hawker the police were on their way up. He knew he had to hurry.

Quickly he went through the pockets of the three corpses. He didn't know why Saul Beckerman had been killed, but it had all the signs of a professional job.

Hawker didn't like professional killers. But he had even less affection for the organizations that hired them.

Hawker had spent the last year fighting such organizations. With the help of his wealthy friend, Jacob Montgomery Hayes, he had, in fact, dedicated himself to fighting any group, anywhere in the country, that preyed on innocent people.

Saul Beckerman hadn't been a close friend. But, in an odd way, he had won Hawker's respect. Saul's note had said he wanted to see Hawker on important business.

This business? The business that had ended his life?

Maybe. No—*probably*. Beckerman had known Hawker's reputation as a tough cop. The best, until he resigned because of all the bureaucratic bullshit that made dealing effectively and legally with crooks and killers damn near impossible.

Beckerman had known . . . he was in trouble, and he had also known that Hawker might be the one individual who could help him.

So this was to be Hawker's assignment: save Saul Beckerman from unknown killers for unknown reasons.

Hawker hadn't even been hired, and already the assignment was blown.

But it wasn't too late for Hawker to go after the organization that had hired the killers.

Retained by a dead man?

Sure, Hawker thought as he surveyed the three corpses. *Why not?*

Sometimes justice was the most demanding employer of all.

Quickly he went through their pockets. Money. Cigarettes. No identification.

They had been careful. Damn careful. It was to be expected. They were professionals.

But in the jacket pocket of the Irishman, Hawker did find something. It was a crumpled piece of paper. On the paper were written two names and two addresses.

One was Saul Beckerman.

The other was a name that stunned Hawker.

It was James O'Neil of 2221 Archer Street.

Jimmy O'Neil was James Hawker's best friend. . . .

JOSEPH WAMBAUGH

Let a brilliant ex-cop take you into the brutal, *real* world of big-city police.